# TEN

## MY BROTHER'S BEST FRIEND

# KER DUKEY

*Ten*
Copyright © 2015 Ker Dukey

All rights reserved. No part of this book may be reproduced or transmitted in any form without written permission of the author.

This book is the work of fiction. Any resemblance to any person alive or dead is purely coincidental. The characters and story are created from the author's imagination. Any shared files without the author's permission will be subject to prosecution.

ISBN-13: 978-1516941971
ISBN-10: 1516941977

WARNING

This title is not as dark as my others but still contains some distressing scenes that could act as triggers for the sensitive reader. Please read with caution.

# DEDICATION

For my patient, amazing readers - thank you for all your continued support and love for my stories.

Love tests us, but those of us truly deserving of it fight for the right to find it, feel it, and keep it.

**Ten years old I fell in love.**
**Ten years was the price of that love.**
**Ten years later our world's re-collide.**

*My brother, Jonah, was possessive when it came to the things he owned. This unfortunately included the people in his life. The forbidden love between his best friend and me was just that… forbidden. Our families were from different walks of life, and as a sheriff's daughter, being with a Moore's kid would never be tolerated. To my parents, their son and Dalton Moore were on different paths, and their friendship would end as soon as college began, but it was my brother who had a craving for trouble. He was always looking for danger, committing petty crimes and getting away with it because Dalton would take the fall, blackening his already stained name. When Jonah found out we broke the rules by loving each other, his actions impacted us all causing immeasurable suffering. Betrayal comes with a debt, and it would be paid by all of us. One with their heart, one with their mind, and one would pay in blood.*

# TEN

(MY BROTHER'S BEST FRIEND)

THE MEN BY NUMBERS SERIES

# CHAPTER ONE

## Soul Mates

### Alexandria (Alex)

*oul mates.* Not everyone believes they exist, but that's because they've never met theirs.

How can someone who has never felt a connection so fierce that they feel the power of it in every molecule of their being believe such a thing can exist?

How can you explain to them that the jolt that ignites every nerve ending in your body is like the sky crackling and exploding with lightning before it joins with the earth for the briefest, yet most magnificent of moments, displaying the true force of nature's power?

When that one person you were created with comes into your life, you know without any doubt that they're yours and you are theirs. It's nature in its truest form.

There is nothing more natural than falling in love with your soul mate. It's like an out of body experience. You transcend before crashing back into your body, seeing life through new eyes.

You don't just find your soul mate; you reunite with them with intensity so powerful nothing can stop it. A love so potent you feel it in the atmosphere, and you see it in their aura.

Dalton Moore was my soul mate and I lived to love him.

He was in my every childhood memory, every dream I conjured.

He was every good decision I made.

But for him…

I was in his every childhood memory, every nightmare he slipped into.

I was the worst decision he ever made.

# CHAPTER TWO

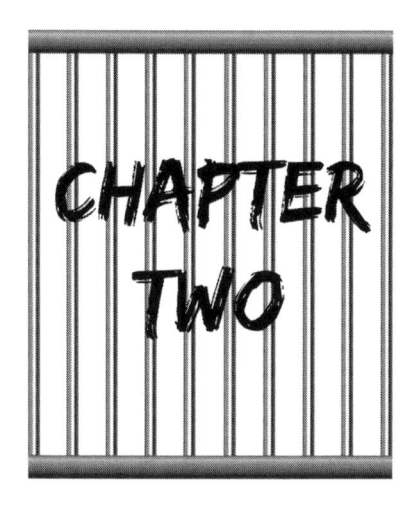

## *Home*

# Alexandria

The knots I knew would come twist my stomach as the *Welcome to Point Meadow* sign appears after the many miles I traveled to get here.

It's surreal being back here after ten years. At one point I never dreamed of leaving here, but in an instant life can change. One minute you're bathing in the warm embrace of the sun, and then without warning, a blizzard comes, distorting and swallowing everything that was once so clear.

Life can grant things like love, happiness, and success, but also evil, destruction, and spite. Each one has graced my life at some point in time.

Pulling up to the house I grew up in, pain seizes my chest. The yard is overgrown and shields the window to my bedroom.

*The one Dalton used to climb through.*

Memories of him pull and twist at my mind causing my soul to silently cry out in pain.

Inhaling a quivering breath, I still my hands from shaking; a reaction that always accompanies thoughts of him. My eyes scan the familiar houses lining the street; they look the same, unchanged by time. No feeling of comfort douses me. Instead, anger and regret saturate my heart.

Bringing the focus back to my childhood home, I grip the keys tighter in my hand, letting the pinch of pain bring me back to my reason for coming back here. The blue paint is peeling and the wraparound porch has been exposed to a cold winter, leaving it battered and untamed. Of all the houses lining the street, Dad's is the one that looks neglected - a far cry from how house proud both he and Mom were when she lived here. My heart hurts to think of Dad living in these conditions.

Less than thirty-six hours ago I received the phone call that my Dad had passed. I didn't even know he was sick. I never understood why he stayed here, or why we let him. I knew he was upset with the way things played out for me but he wasn't the type of man - the type of father - who would turn his back on his child or his family, so I knew there was more to it, but Mom was tight-lipped and refused to talk about it.

Everything was so muddled for me back then. I was

sixteen when I was shipped away with Mom and Jonah, my life changing forever in a blink of an eye.

*"He's poison, just like the rest of them. I told you to stay away from the Moore's boy. He's trash, Alexandria. Trash, trash, trash."*

Mom's harsh words echo around the empty space surrounding me, and even though it's a phantom sound from a memory ten years old, I still find myself covering my ears with the palms of my hands, just like I did back then.

I will myself to move and stop thinking about everything that happened back then, but it's hard, I feel like I've been trapped there my whole life, struggling to move on. I never understood why Dalton never reached out to me, never let me see him. I gained something magical from our love and will cherish that for the rest of my life, even if he doesn't, but the pain of losing that sweet, precious kind of love that can't be replaced is as strong as the first night I spent thousands of miles away from him.

I grab the suitcase and boxes from the trunk and fight my way through the weeds up the garden path, inhaling a breath to prepare myself as I unlock the front door. Mail and old newspapers lie in a layer of dust just inside the entranceway. Pushing the door farther open creates a cloud of dirt around me. The musky scent hits me in the face causing a coughing fit. I want to cry but I promised myself I'd be strong and do what needs to be done then get back to my life - the life I was sent away to live. *Was I living?*

Seeing the dust and the amount of mail collected, I

realize he must not have been staying here for a while. Maybe he was in the hospital for a long time. Why didn't someone call us?

I'd missed him over the years. He was a fantastic father, even in the moments when he'd tried to keep me away from Dalton. It was hard to come to terms with him not being with Mom. I blamed myself and the situation I'd gotten myself into, even though I knew Jonah's drug problem played a huge part.

I hate the dark spots, the blank explanations I got from Mom. I don't think she will ever be honest with me about what happened, and I still can't talk to Jonah since that day. He tries calling, and sends cards and letters. He never misses a birthday, and I do wonder what he's like now. But the version of him in my bedroom ten years ago can't be erased from my mind, so I stay far away from him.

I drop my luggage on the table before walking to the window and drawing the curtains open. I still my thoughts of fleeing and get on with it. Dalton's house glares at me from across the street, mocking me through the pane of glass.

Dalton came to live with his uncle when his father went to prison for murder. The Moore family was well known to my Daddy, the town's sheriff, but to me, at ten years old, Dalton Moore was just a boy, and I was just a girl completely smitten with the older boy across the street. I remember the first day I ever saw him. The sun was so hot that day, and Mom and slathered my skin in sunscreen. I didn't mind, I was used to her over-protective manner,

## TEN

and the screen smelled sweet like coconut. It was one of the first things Dalton ever said to me.

*"You smell so sweet. Like coconut cake."*

# Chapter Three

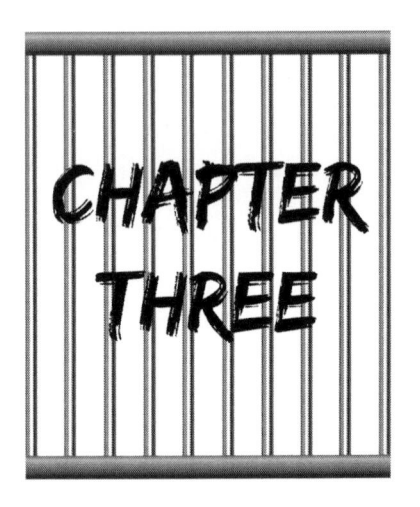

## *First glance*

# Alexandria

I remember Mom rushing in with the morning paper; I was sitting at the breakfast table watching Jonah shovel in Lucky Charms. He was so gross. The milk dripping down his chin onto his clean shirt made Dad's eyes roll and frown lines crease his forehead, but Mom was insistent he was going through a growth spurt and needed extra calories, so we all refrained from commenting on his pig-like behavior. It's funny the things you remember, and usually I don't remember whole days in such detail, but this day was the day from which my life would never be the same again.

## **TEN**

## TEN YEARS AGO

*"There's a moving truck over at the Moore's house," Mom shouted to Dad, walking in and frantically pacing between the table and the kitchen window that overlooked our front yard.*

*Dad jumped up from the table to stare out the window with her. He was ready for work, his uniform crease-free, and it fit him perfectly. The sheriff badge sat proud on his breast. My Dad was a hero in my young eyes; he looked after the whole town and everyone looked up to him. Well, all except Jonah, who hated being the sheriff's son and made it his life's mission to get into trouble wherever possible.*

*When he was nine years old, Jonah stole candy from our local sweetshop. Daddy made him work there after school for a month to repay Mrs. Gibson, but it didn't stop Jonah from getting into more trouble. He knew that no matter what he did, he would never get into real police trouble because his Dad was the police. He used to steal milk from doorsteps every morning after the milkman had been, and put wet mud in mailboxes. It was all prank-type behavior, but his juvenile crimes evolved with age. One time he took me to the park, and when a boy pushed me too high on the swings causing me to fall and bust my knees and lip, he flew into a rage, hitting the boy until he fell to the ground in a fetal position. He then threw the boy's bike into the road in front of a car, which nearly caused the car to crash. Dad was more concerned with my injuries than what Jonah had done.*

*Mom made Jonah this way with me. She told Jonah*

*every time we left the house together that I was his responsibility, his soul mate, and that he had to take good care of me. She used to tell us stories of my birth, how I didn't cry when I was born. She believes it's because I was happy to be here, that I was supposed to be here, with Jonah. She told us I had severe colic, and that I cried constantly in pain until Jonah sat beside my cot and stroked my tummy. She was convinced only his presence would soothe me. Jonah loved hearing those stories and took them all to heart, which made life difficult for me. He was over-protective and mean to anyone who wanted to play with me, which meant when he wasn't around I, spent a lot of time on my own.*

"*It's a small truck for removals, honey,*" *Dad said, chomping down on a piece of toast and washing it down with black coffee that made his kisses smell like he ate the stuff straight from the jar. I remember bouncing on my seat trying to look over them out the window, but Mom blocked the view.*

"*It doesn't matter how big the truck is, as long as we get rid of that awful Keith. I hate that I have to look at him every day.*"

*Keith Moore had always lived across from us. The house used to belong to his wife, Marie; it was left to her in her folks' will. She married Keith just before I was born but Mom always had something to say whenever she saw the duo.*

"Her mother would turn in her grave if she knew her daughter fished at the bottom of the pool and scraped the dirt off the bottom."

"He only married her for the house so he can mock us."

## TEN

*"Why can't he just overdose already?"*

*Marie was a quiet woman who wore huge sunglasses to cover up the bruises on her face. One day I woke early, anxious for the first day of school, and saw her loading her car with suitcases in a hurry before getting in the car and driving away. I never saw her again. I overheard Dad telling Mom she was in New York now and was never coming back. Mom was thrilled, hoping it meant Keith would have to move, but he didn't. She left him the house and everything inside but her clothes. Dad had tried to help her when he saw she had new bruises but she was terrified of her husband; even I could sense it, and I never knew much about the emotion until I got older.*

"Well, I'll find out what's happening today. Now kiss me, I have to go to work."

*My nose scrunched, knowing she would be getting a coffee kiss, and I'd be next.*

*After Dad left for work, Mom told me to go play outside while she spoke to Jonah. I'd been out in the yard for five minutes. I'd just buckled my roller skates into place when the removal van pulled away giving me a full view of the Moore's house, and on the top step stood a boy. My heart did a funny flip; I've been searching for that same feeling for the last ten years but I've never felt the impact of another's soul like I did that day. I still feel it when I think of the moment I first saw him. I revisit the memory just to touch the feeling, if only for a fleeting moment.*

*Light blond hair lay in chaos over his head, drooping low into the clearest blue eyes I'd ever seen. I couldn't move, and when he noticed me, time appeared to stop. I would have believed my heart stopped beating in that moment if I hadn't felt it frantically pounding in my chest.*

*Ten years old, but I knew what was happening went beyond our innocence. Age didn't matter; it was fate. It was souls realigning and engaging each other.*

*Mom talked about soul mates my whole life. She believed that soul mates didn't have to be your husband or wife, but you could find them in a friend or sibling, and she constantly told Jonah I was his and he had to look after me.* How wrong she was.

*A shadow fell over my body and the boy's eyes came into focus as he said, "You smell so sweet. Like coconut cake. Have you been baking?"*

*I couldn't speak for a minute, but he grinned down at me then took my hands in his and helped me to stand on my skates.*

*"I'm Dalton. I just moved in with my uncle."*

*"I'm Jonah," came the booming voice of my brother, breaking our connection by tugging my hands from Dalton's. "She's my sister and she's only ten."*

*Dalton's eyes bulged slightly. He stepped away from me and I hated my brother in that moment. He was thirteen and going through a phase where he was beginning to date girls, so he thought all boys thought about girls in the same way he did. As playthings.*

*Jonah and Dalton stood at the same height, and I would have guessed Dalton was the same age as Jonah, but age doesn't matter when it comes to fate, and in a few years that gap wouldn't seem so glaring.*

*When my Dad came home and informed Mom our*

## TEN

*street had gained a Moore instead of losing one, and the reason he was there, she forbid both Jonah and I to have anything to do with the new boy. Jonah wasn't one for following rules, and I followed his lead. There was nothing that would keep me from Dalton. I was infatuated.*

*Things got better for me when Dalton moved in across the street. He and Jonah got on brilliantly and eventually Jonah trusted Dalton around me and let me tag along with them when they went out on their bikes, or swimming in the lake. We were a trio and I loved it, because even that young, I loved Dalton Moore more than I loved anything. He made me laugh with his cute humor and mannerisms. He was caring and gentle, with a beautiful nature. Generous and gracious was part of Dalton's daily routine. Despite how rude my Mom could be, he always had a smile and a polite word for her.*

*He worked hard in school and was a huge hockey fan. He played for our school team and took it insanely seriously. That was his dream - to leave the Moore name behind him and have a professional hockey career. He was good enough for that, too. Jonah also played on the team but was more a relaxed player, skipping practices, and trying to encourage Dalton to do the same, but Dalton was extremely focused. When he wasn't consumed with practice he spent all of his time with us, and I craved his company. When I wasn't around him for a long period of time, I became sullen and lonely, which I know isn't healthy, but it was just the way he made me feel when I was around him. He was like the sun, and I was a flower waiting to bloom in his presence.*

*There were times when I wasn't allowed to go with them*

*on some of the boy trips, and it felt like torture. My hormones in disarray, it made me mad at Jonah for making me a loner. I should have had girlfriends to do things with, but I didn't. I had those two and no one else.*

*Jonah used to sneak out at night and climb the big tree outside Dalton's bedroom window. I hated when he did that. I could see Dalton's room from my own and we spent many nights writing messages to each other by holding up pieces of paper with words written in bold black marker, but on the nights Jonah climbed that tree, moments later they would both climb back down and be gone for the night. I never knew where they went or what they got up to, but I was jealous I wasn't involved.*

"You're younger than us, Alex. There's things you don't understand yet, and things I don't want you to know about."

*Dalton's words hurt because I knew what those things were. Lisa Marie made it her mission to let the whole female population of our school know she used to meet up with Dalton, that she was his girlfriend and they did things, things I was too young to do for him. It slashed at me like a whip every time I heard the rumors. One night I saw her outside his house. She was giggling, trying to climb the tree up to his room - the tree he had been teaching me to climb. My heart felt heavy in my chest. Emotions are so intensified when you're young. It felt like the world would end on so many occasions through my awkward years, waiting to be old enough for Dalton. He angrily shouted down at her from his window, and then seconds later appeared at his*

## TEN

*door, hurrying her inside. I hid behind my curtain when I felt his eyes scan my window. I was twelve and heartbroken. My soul suffered so much in the early years; it was scratching to tear from my body and rush to him. I wanted to be old enough for him. I would have let him do anything he wanted with me, old enough or not. I was his and he mine.*

*I'd asked him if the rumors were true, and he stroked my cheek and laughed.*

"Don't believe everything girls talk about, Alex, but believe me when I tell you that when you're old enough, I'm going to marry you."

*My spirit felt lighter at his words but soon grew heavy when Jonah walked up behind me, and Dalton snatched his hand back so fast it was as if my flesh rebuked him. His friendship with Jonah was more important to him than us being together. I'd waited so patiently and feared I'd always be waiting for Dalton Moore to really see me.*

*I made it my mission to learn how to climb that damn tree, and to never let Jonah stop me from marrying Dalton Moore.*

# CHAPTER FOUR

## *Pain*

## Alexandria

I quickly shake away the memories trying to drown me and slide the windows wide to get some air in this place. All the furniture is the same, only more worn. *How could we have left him like this?*

I notice one of Dad's sweaters on the back of his armchair and a tear leaks onto my cheek. My feet carry me across the room and I pick it up, inhaling his scent. *It smells the same as he always did.* This was going to be harder than I first thought. I wish I'd taken Leon up on his offer to come with me. I met him when I moved into my apartment building; he was my neighbor, and extremely loud. I'd put up with the music for the first couple of nights, but by night three I was going to tear my hair out. I banged so hard on his wall that he came to my door carrying the broken picture that had fallen at the vibrations of my fist. My hair was all over the place and I was wearing odd PJs with no bra underneath, and I only had on one sock. The smirk on his face made my blood boil. I was sleep deprived and exhausted.

"You know, you could have just knocked and asked me to keep it down." His brow rose with a cocky charm. His eyes were a cinnamon chocolate color, cased in thick, dark lashes. He was fully dressed in jeans and a hoody with "4am wakeup call" slashed across the front.

"I didn't think you'd hear me over the noise," I all but growled at him.

"But hammering on the wall and shouting, and I quote, '*Shut the hell up or I'm going to stick that guitar where the sun doesn't shine, mister,*' you thought I'd hear just fine?"

I shrugged a shoulder, a little embarrassed at my actions and attire.

"Well, clearly you did." A yawn erupted from my mouth at the end of my sentence, causing a chuckle to bubble up through his.

"Listen, I had no idea anyone had moved in here. I've been living here alone for months. I'll keep the noise down if you promise to keep from ruining anymore pictures, deal?"

"Deal, and I'll replace your frame." I grabbed the picture from him and shut the door before he could react. I didn't want him to think I was a bad neighbor, and I hated that I'd broken someone else's property.

I replaced the frame the next day and left it for him outside his apartment so I didn't have to see him again; I was still a little embarrassed. He thanked me by leaving a bottle of wine outside my door. I plucked up the courage to come out of my shell and knocked on his door to ask if he wanted to share a glass with me so we could have a fresh start. We became great friends and have been for years now, but as with most things, I had to go and mess it up. Everything is complicated now.

I'd let the grief of Dad's passing overwhelm me. I gave in to the affection he'd shown me. We slept together and then I left to come straight here before talking about what happened. I was a selfish bitch. I know Leon has more than friendly feelings for me, and after seven years of not acting on them, he made a move when I was in a vulnerable state, and I scavenged for it like a starved-for-affection ho. Now things are awkward, or they will be when I have to talk to him next. The truth is I can't be without him. He's my rock and I need him. *We* need him so this is going to have to be handled delicately.

*So you run away without speaking to him?*

Damn, I hate my conscience.

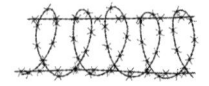

This place is disgusting, I need to at least clean a bedroom and a bathroom before anything else, so I have somewhere to sleep and shower. Looking under the basin where cleaning supplies should be, I'm not surprised to find nothing but an old bucket and a plunger. I'll have to

## TEN

go to the store, which, considering how hungry I am isn't a bad thing.

As I leave the house, my feet still. Dalton's old home directly opposite is in perfect view and memories threaten to rip my heart from my chest once again. The garden is kept tidy and groomed and the paintwork is fresh. The sight of the tall tree to the side of the house nearly makes my knees buckle.

*"You can totally climb it, Alex. Be brave. I won't let you fall."*

But he did let me fall. He let me fall in love, and although I was just a child in the eyes of my parents, I've never known a feeling like it since. It's still there under all of the damage, thumping a soft thud, waiting to be awakened again.

I wonder who lives there now.

The drive into town is full of nostalgia. Everything is the same, but different in subtle ways. The car lot has a new name, and the cinema now stretches across two shop fronts instead of just one, but it's still where I grew up. I can almost feel the fifteen-year-old me tearing out of my skin, asking for a do over. I hate living with regret, but I do, and it's toxic inside me.

By the time I pull into the store parking lot, the sun is beginning to set, causing a warm orange glow to cast over the entire town. This time of night always reminds me of the long summer nights, riding our bikes and believing the world was made for us, and that dreams were free. Dreams are not free, and they cost us dearly.

I recognize the cashier as soon as I load my groceries onto the checkout counter. We went to school together. Lacy Holbrook - she was ditzy and fun in class, but we didn't hang out much outside of school. She had a crush on Jonah, who embarrassed her at a party by letting her give him oral sex and then later that night, he slept with her best friend. She cried right in front of him and he cruelly laughed at her. He was so mean to girls. He used them freely because most offered themselves that way. He had no respect for girls apart from me, and that gave him a bad boy reputation, and me the reputation of the bad boy's goody-two-shoes little sister. I didn't date, not that I could have with Jonah as a brother, but it was because I was in love with Dalton. I didn't have many people who really called me a friend, but Lacy, despite the way Jonah treated her, was nice to me and let me sit with her at lunch, and partner up with her for studying when the age barrier didn't come in to play.

I don't say anything because I'm a little embarrassed that she won't recognize or remember me. I load everything into bags and wait for the total, and that's when she looks up at me with a huge fuchsia-coated smile. Her jaw drops. "Oh my God, Alex!" She screeches, leaning over the counter to hug me. I welcome her affection and return it with my own hug. "I haven't seen you around these parts for years. What are you doing here?"

"My Dad passed. I came to arrange things." I can't return her enthusiasm; the truth of why I'm here isn't happy.

"Oh, darn. Sorry to hear that, sweetie. How long are you in town?"

I shrug and hand her some bills.

## TEN

"I get off in an hour. Come grab some food with me?"

I'm starving and cooking isn't something I feel like doing.

"Okay, sure."

"Great! Meet me at Bernie's diner in an hour."

# CHAPTER FIVE

## *New Places, Old Faces*

### Alexandria

I unpack the few things I bought and start cleaning my old bathroom. Before I know it, the hour has flown by and I need to clean up before meeting Lacy. I dress casually and make sure I have some cash in my purse before taking off.

My stomach growls as I enter the diner, the aroma of fried food thick in the air - just what I need. I can't remember the last time I ate so I order extra fries with my burger and onion rings to fill me for the night, and probably the start of tomorrow.

Lacy soon joins me, looking like she's going to a nightclub not a diner.

## TEN

"Did you go home?" I ask, looking her over and then down at myself. She's wearing killer heels that would make my legs buckle, a mini skirt that - if she bent over - would make the old man staring at her stroke out, and a halter top that shows more cleavage than it covers up.

She waves her hand dismissively. "God, no. I keep this in my locker for special occasions."

"I'm a special occasion?" I raise a brow, skeptical.

"Damn right you are! We're going to catch up on all the years we missed together."

"Okay. I just ordered." I point to the waitress flitting from one table to the next.

"Not here, silly. I need tequila." She grins, dragging me from my chair and out the door.

I'm starving and almost resort to grabbing onto the doorframe to prevent her getting me out without food inside me, but I could also use a drink, and maybe girl talk will make a nice change.

She drags me to Numbers; a bar that's been in this town longer than both of us, only the name has changed. It used to be Mack's Bar. I prop myself on the bar stool and take in the atmosphere. It looks completely different to how I remember it. Granted, I only ever saw inside through the windows, but still, the bar has undergone a major makeover. The new owners must have invested time and money into the place.

"So what are you having?"

"I'm driving so I'll just stick to a white wine spritzer and then soft drinks," I tell her.

She rolls her eyes at me. "I'll get Mason to pick us up

and drop you home. It's your first night back, girl! Let's celebrate."

"Mason?"

"Mason Jones. You remember him, right?"

My eyes widen slightly. "The Mathlete?"

Mason was unfortunate in the looks department; he had fuzzy blond curly hair, thick-rimmed glasses, and braces to boot. His skin was covered in pimples and he spent most of his time locked in a classroom, studying. He was polite and a great kid, but if there was ever a cliché for geek, he was it.

"Yeah, that Mason. Well, he shed that whole ugly look and I bone him from time to time." She shrugs like she just admitted to making him dinner.

She waves the bartender over with a *come hither* crook of her finger. He grins and nods his head towards her. "Hey, Lacy. What can I get you?"

"Tequila shots!"

"Who's your new friend?" He gestures with a not-so-subtle nod.

She bounces in her seat and slaps her palm on the bar. If I didn't know better I'd think she'd been here a while and was already intoxicated. "Not new, old. This is Alex Murphy. We were childhood friends."

Before any of us can say anything else, the stool I'm sitting on gives way under the foot kicking the bottom of it out from under me. My arms flail, a startled scream wrenches from my chest, and my head hits the floor with a thud. I can't focus on the man standing over me; my eyesight is blurred.

When my equilibrium returns I notice the music has

## TEN

stopped and the entire bar is silent. An angry sneer coming from a man I don't recognize causes my heart to beat painfully in my chest. *Why is no one helping me?*

Life as I know it slows and then fast forwards like I've swallowed the "Drink Me" bottle from *Alice in Wonderland* and I'm tumbling down the rabbit hole. Everything is mute, and there's a fierce atmosphere sucking the once happy vibes from the place.

I feel like I'm being pulled through a black hole. Every part of my existence is being tugged and torn until there will be nothing left of me but particles screaming to be whole again.

My insides heat and tingle, every molecule twisting and splintering. I'm not going to make it through the other side of whatever this is, not whole anyway. Everything will come back together but I won't be the same. Part of me will be lost here and never recovered because his face appears.

*Dalton.*

# CHAPTER SIX

## *This Can't Be Real*

## Alexandria

Dalton appears next to the man who kicked my stool out.

Everything good and beautiful is gone from his eyes, like an eclipse happened inside him and the dark blocked out any light and warmth of the former host; my soul mate, my Dalton.

"She has some nerve, Ten! You can't let her be here. It's disrespectful."

*Ten?*

The sound of fist hitting flesh and bone makes me gag. I'm dizzy from the fall and I can feel blood seeping into my hair from the hit I took to the head.

## TEN

The man's nose crumbles under the impact of Dalton's fist, and blood leaks freely, staining the clothes he's wearing.

"You don't cause a scene like this in my place, or tell me what to do. You take it out back. I won't tell you again." Dalton growls.

He towers over the smaller man who doesn't try to fight back, and I don't blame him. Dalton's tall, imposing frame alone is frightening, but the scowl on such a beautiful canvas is haunting. His full lips curl into sneer as he reaches down and drags me to my unsteady feet. The pinch of his long, thick fingers in the top of my small arm makes me gasp in pain. Murmurs from around the bar follow us until we reach a fire exit. He uses a heavy palm to open the door, and it nearly swings back and hits me, but the force of his grip and hurried pace has me hurtling forward before it has the chance. I can't prevent myself from colliding with the wet concrete outside the door. A burning sensation ignites my knees and the palms of my hands. I'd only just managed to put my hands out in front of me, preventing further head injury. It takes my mind time to catch up with the reality of what's happening.

*Dalton is here. Dalton just threw you to the ground in a wet, trash-filled ally.*

Turning my body to look up at the man who hurled me to the floor, I almost vomit

The ferocity of his anger brings a sickening tremor to my body. I'm scared of him. The boy who owns my soul is lost inside the eyes of the stranger standing over me.

"Dalton?" I manage to breathe, making him flinch.

The door re-opening gains my attention but not his.

His eyes cling to me, undoing ten years of me trying to be a woman who doesn't need to love him. With just one look, I'm that ten-year-old girl, captivated by the azure eyes that flashed with energy every time they saw me.

"I can't believe it's her," came the voice of the person who has joined us.

I recognize her straight away; Lisa Marie. The same long golden blonde hair sweeps neatly over her slender shoulders. Her oval face holds delicate features, but she's a wolf in a princess' clothing. All through high school she was a bitch. Older than me by two years, and the girl I hated more than anyone. Her willowy frame steps forward, and before I can protect myself, her leg kicks out and her boot collides with my face. Shock freezes me. I can't move to get away; I just lie here in pain. The warm trickle of blood from my mouth makes me gag and hurl bile to the ground. The blood against the cold rain thundering down on me scares me. There's a lot, so I know I'm cut. A tug on my hair whips my head back and I prepare myself for another assault, but before Lisa can hit me again she's tugged away by Dalton.

"Get off me! After everything she took from you, Ten, I'm going to kill her."

There was that name again. Ten.

*What I took from him?*

He didn't want anything to do with me. He never answered my letters.

"Get in! Now!" he roars, pushing her towards the exit door we left through.

"I'll be seeing you, bitch." She spits in my direction before sauntering inside.

# TEN

Dalton's heavy frame turns back to me and I wilt under the intensity of the anger radiating from him. "You shouldn't have come here. Who the fuck do you think you are? I don't ever want to see you here again, because next time I won't pull anyone off you. I'll let them give you what you deserve."

*What I deserve?*

Cold rain seeps into my clothes and over my exposed skin, dampening my hair and causing it to stick to my face. I welcome the downpour; it obscures the tears falling from my eyes. I don't want him to see me crying, to see me broken by his harsh, cruel words and behavior.

His stance emphasizes the raw power of his muscular body, the rain quickly drenching the cotton tee he's wearing, showing the contours of his shoulders and chest, and as much as I'm hurting, the visual still quickens my pulse. His once bright blond hair is darker, and has lost its shape. Drops of rain bubble on his steel set jaw. He carries himself with a commanding confidence that makes me cower inside myself, preventing me from doing what I want to do.

I want to jump up and pummel my small fists into his chest, and scream at him.

*"It's me! It's me! You loved me once and I will always love you! Don't treat me this way. How dare you? You're my soul mate. You're my soul mate, God damn you!"* But my worst fear is playing out in front of me, and the way he peers down at me like I'm the trash he just threw out curdles my soul. He really doesn't care who I am or what we once shared. He's a different person now and he's forgotten me. *Worse. He remembers me and he hates me.*

Getting to my feet, I sway unsteadily, feeling nauseous. My face throbs from Lisa's boot, and it causes anger to fire up inside me, my blood rages as my heart pounds heavily. I will never be a victim like this, not again.

I should have protected myself, defended myself, but I couldn't comprehend everything that was happening, and it all happened so fast.

I use the wall to support myself and hobble down the alley with Dalton's eyes burning a scar into my back. I was right. I'll never be the same again.

I make it to my car and sobs burst from my chest. Patting down my damp, sore body, I learn my bag with my keys in is still on the bar. I want to scream into the rain but not be heard, and I know that's not an option. Getting inside my car to get away from here as quickly as possible is what I need to do. Noticing a police car through the blur of my tears, I debate reporting the abuse I was just put through, but despite the pain in my heart over Dalton, I don't want to bring attention to how he treated me or allowed others to treat me.

"Alex," Lacy's cautious tone calls out. "Oh, God. Look at you." She shakes her head in sympathy, but I don't need that from her. I needed her to help me when I was in the bar, but instead, like everyone else, she stood in silence.

"I brought your bag."

I snatch my purse from her grasp and fumble inside for my car keys.

"I'm sorry, Alex," she mumbles.

I turn, the anger raging to the surface. "Why didn't you help me or get help? Why did no one help me in there?"

Shaking her head, she reaches to place her hands on my shoulders but I shrug her off. "It's a Moore's bar. It was a Moore, Alex. No one would dare, or bad things would happen to them too. I'm so sorry."

I unlock my car and hastily jump in, turning the heating on full to warm my skin and dry off, but the drive back to my old home is done while feeling completely cold, and completely numb.

When I pull up, I run into the house, locking the door before sliding down it to the floor. My body trembles as the floods of emotion overwhelm me. I curl into a ball and let myself cry. I don't know how long I lie there but my cell chiming pulls me from my misery. When I see that it's DJ, I quickly swipe my tears and take a few deep breaths

"Hello, sweetie."

"Hey. I know it's late but I just wanted to say goodnight."

"Missing me already, huh?"

"Always, but Leon is so cool, so don't worry about me. He took me shopping for my new guitar."

"That's wonderful, baby. I miss you so much already. I don't plan to stay here long."

"Are you crying?"

"No, silly. I'm just tired. It's been a long few days."

"Okay. I love you, Mom."

"I love you too, baby. Goodnight."

Hearing from my son, *our* son, only makes my heart crumble more. Dropping the phone to the floor, I lie amongst the dirt. Physically, I am here. Mentally I'm far, far away.

# CHAPTER SEVEN

## *First Time*

## Alexandria

*I was fourteen when I had my first kiss. I'd mastered climbing Dalton's tree years before, and when he didn't sneak through my bedroom window to spend the night, I snuck out and climbed the tree into his room. He wasn't there once I made it up, so I curled up in his bed to wait for him.*

*I awoke to a noise from outside his window, and I saw him kissing Lisa goodbye. My world came crashing down around me. He always told me that he would make me his as soon as I was old enough, and that we would get married and never be apart, but if I had to wait, why couldn't he? I despised Lisa and every touch she got that I didn't. My soul*

## TEN

*cried every time she spoke about him in the locker room or in the lunch hall. It felt like a betrayal that he went to her. Why did he do that if he didn't love her?*

*I swiped the tears soaking my cheeks and waited for him to come up to his room. It was ten minutes before he appeared. I startled him and he stumbled a little and looked around his room and then to the window sheepishly.*

*"Alex, what are you doing in here?"*

*"Waiting for you," I croaked out. Anger and irrational thoughts churned inside me. "I love you," I spat out into the room, and nervously stepped from foot to foot while playing with a loose piece of thread dangling from my shirt. "I loved you the first time I saw you, and you know I do. You promised me that you'll marry me, and you think I'm a little girl who will be content with that. Well, guess what, Dalton Moore? I'm not."*

*His eyes grew wide at my words and he walked closer to me, warning me to quiet down with hand gestures and frantic head nodding towards his bedroom door but I was too mad to listen to him.*

*"I hate Lisa. I hate that you do things with her. I hate that she talks about it all around school. I hate that you tell me I'm special and that we will be together one day, but all the time you're with her and I'm alone."*

*"You're only fourteen, Alex. Your brother would never let us be together."*

*"Well, maybe he doesn't get a say, Dalton. Or maybe you never meant those things you said, and really you just don't want to hurt your best friend's sister who is crushing on you."*

*"Now you're talking crazy and you know it. If you were*

*just a little older... It's so hard for me, Alex. Your brother wouldn't understand, and your parents, God... your Dad would arrest me!"*

*"Now who's talking crazy? Maybe I am a little young. Maybe I should date boys my own age," I teased, to see if I could gage a reaction. He stood silent and still so I pushed a little more. "Jordon Reese told me he wanted to give me my first kiss today, and asked if I would go out with him this weekend." It was the truth. Jordon was new and didn't know my brother...yet.*

*Dalton's heavy footfalls stomped across his room until he stood a fraction away from me. His large hands encased my face. His eyes were heavy-lidded and there was a mist in them, highlighting the powerful blue. "I'll be your first kiss. Your first everything. Please, Alex. Just wait for me."*

*I felt his plea through the intensity of his gaze. I dropped my tone so he knew I was more sad than angry. "I'm done waiting while watching you do it without me."*

*His forehead came down to rest against mine and he closed his eyes and inhaled heavily.*

*"I love you too. Since the first day I saw you." His lips smoothed over mine, eliciting a small gasp of surprise. His mouth slowly coaxed mine to open and his warm tongue slid delicately into my mouth. It was weird, warm and soft, but as his tongue pushed firmer against my lips, my own joined his to form a dance, and it felt incredible. When he eventually pulled away I groaned in disappointment.*

*"That's all I can give you for now. That, and a promise that I'm done with Lisa and any other girl. You will wait for me and I'll wait for you, and as soon as you're old enough we will be together." A sigh of relief pushed past my lips and*

## TEN

*I willed the tears threatening to fall to dissipate.*

*And I did wait, and he gave me all my firsts. He was the first person to make love to me, and the first person to break my heart.*

# CHAPTER EIGHT

*Hate*

## Dalton (Ten)

I dream about her scent on my pillows, her soft innocent laughter echoing through my room as I tickle her supple body into submission. Sweet, innocent, faithful Alex.

That person doesn't really exist, yet she's more real in my dreams than she is here. People always try to tell me how to act, how I should feel, what revenge I need to take, but they don't know what it was like for me. They're not me and I'm not them, or at least, I wasn't. All I ever wanted was to get out of this town and shed the family name which is more a curse then an inheritance. Instead, here I am, the exact thing I promised myself I'd never be, and

## TEN

that makes my blood run cold.

My soul had floated above my body, looking in at a scene but not really being a part of it when the commotion in the bar broke out. I didn't expect to see her back here, but there she was, sprawled out on the floor like she just fell from a forbidden apple tree. She was different but the same all in one glance... if that's even possible.

She's grown. Damn, she's grown, but her eyes and lips still hold the traits of the young girl I fell in love with. She does this thing where, when she smiles, it's like she can smile with her whole face. It reaches her eyes; they do this glistening, sparkling shit that grips me by the balls and turns me into her bitch. *I'm not that boy anymore.*

Reality hit me full force when I came back to myself. My feet had carried me to her. What a fucking bitch. How dare she come back here and into my bar?

Her hair lay fanned around her delicately curved facial features. She now has blonde streaks, making her dark brown eyes appear even darker. She whimpered as I dragged her to her feet, but fuck, I couldn't, no, I *wouldn't* act weak just because it was her, and seeing her for the first time came with a feeling of such intense shock my whole body lit up with nervous energy, making it hard to focus. I'd imagined seeing her again over and over, but nothing could have prepared me for that look in her eye. Love, regret, guilt? *Fuck her!*

Her face was pale with tears threatening, her long eyelashes making them appear unnatural. They were so incredibly long and she has a way of batting them, making her seem innocent, but she's anything but.

She rose quickly to her feet with my hand tightening

around her arm. Her tits have definitely grown with her. They bounced slightly as she moved, and despite my bitter feelings towards her, I'm a man - a man who knows what it's like to be inside that tight little body. My balls tightened so painfully I had to bite the inside of my mouth to stop myself from licking my lips, *or her face.*

She has a slim waist which flares in to curvy hips and thighs that the jeans she wore hugged perfectly. Damn every inch of flesh that caressed those jeans.

Why did she have to come here looking fucking beautiful? To taunt me? Hadn't I suffered enough?

It's funny how one minute you have a million aspirations for your life, and the one person you want with you when you succeed is the one who broke everything, crushed your dreams, and ruined your life. I still hear her screams when I close my eyes. From the day I was dragged away because of her family… because of her.

I got her outside and shoved her towards the alley. I needed her gone. Her body collided with the wet asphalt but I didn't care. I wouldn't. Fuck her.

When Lisa appeared and lashed out, I wanted to knock her out and leave her out with the trash. She oversteps at every opportunity and thinks me fucking her is more than just that, but it isn't. The only reason I fuck her is because Alex hated her all those years ago, so every time I thrust into her wet heat it's a "fuck you" to Alex. Pathetic, like she'd even give a shit, but I feed from the small satisfactions I can get. Lisa also likes it hard and dirty, which is more to my tastes. I'm not one for intimacy. I fuck to relieve stress, and to feel anything but the darkening pit inside my gut swallowing more of me every day. Lisa likes

## TEN

to fuck too. She hasn't changed over the years. She married the first prick who flashed his cash at her. It didn't last long though. He used to go out of town for business, and it turned out he had a whole other life. She divorced him and fucked everything that moved as her way of getting back at him. She's easy, and I'm all about easy these days.

So when she came out and planted herself in the dispute with Alex, it pissed me the fuck off.

Alex was soaking, and the blood on her face confused the boy and the man inside me. I didn't like seeing her that way but I was so livid, and in the same breath turned on by the nipple showing through her wet clothes. She's so fuckable. I had to convince myself hate-fucking her would give her pleasure too, and she doesn't deserve any pleasure from me.

She got to her feet and unsteadily walked away.

I won't worry about her. I won't think about Jude kicking her stool out from under her and her head impacting the floor. I won't think about Lisa's boot connecting with her small, delicate jaw.

I won't think about how I had no one growing up but her. She knew what I'd come from, lived through, and even knowing that she still betrayed me, hurt me… broke me.

My Dad was a violent criminal, my Mom a drug addict who would sell her body to the highest bidder, which included my father when he decided he wanted her back after kicking her out the week before.

One night when I was thirteen she was high and fell asleep with a cigarette lit. She nearly burned down our house with me asleep inside. Dad came home just in time to prevent it but his anger turned into a drunk-fueled rage. Momma never did know when to keep her mouth shut. I came out of my room to him shouting, and I watched from six feet away… too far to stop him as one closed fist to her fragile temple sent her to the floor in a heavy heap; lights out. I'd seen them fight so many times before, and Mom was as bad as Dad for the violence, but I knew this was different. She went down so limply, and my Dad's face contorted in confusion. The girl he brought home with him dialed for an ambulance but Mom was pronounced dead at the scene.

I was taken in by my Dad's brother; he was also the guy who took over running the family business, which I knew from an early age involved heavy drug involvement. The comforting words I got from him when I arrived were, "He should have buried her out the back with the rest of the wildlife. Fucking idiot. I knew she'd be his downfall."

Thirteen years old, lost both parents, and that was what I got. How did I even end up with him? Why wasn't I put in the system or sent to one of my many aunts? It was because my destiny was here, or so I thought. It was back then when I first saw her. *Alex.*

When you think the sun will never shine, and life is lived in the darkness of the night no matter the time of day, then out of nowhere a beacon burns so bright it obliterates all the darkness - that was Alex. She sat on her lawn buckling up her skates, and she had flowing auburn hair and big doe-like eyes that found mine and held me mesmerized. It wasn't a sexual attraction. We were young, and to put what we shared down to that would be weak. It

## TEN

would be unfair to both of us. For me, seeing her for the first time and every time thereafter was like being awoken, finally knowing there was good in my life.

Our connection was formed long before our bodies ever met. We were made for each other, a pair crafted from the same soul. How does the saying go? A match made in heaven? That's what we were, but that match was struck and the flame burned us both.

Anger bubbles and roars out of me, the wall taking the brunt from my fist as I jab a few times, causing my skin to tear and bleed. The rain dilutes the blood pouring from my knuckles and I wish it could weaken the pain, but it's still right there, as vivid as the day it happened.

# Chapter Nine

## Dalton

### Ten Years Ago

*I couldn't believe what Jonah had gotten himself in to. We'd been friends for seven years but we'd been drifting apart, heading in two opposite directions. I couldn't wait to leave this place and start planning my future, which involved telling him I was in love with his baby sister. I'd been putting it off since forever because Jonah was temperamental. There was something missing from him. He'd appeared lonely and beaten down by life ever since I'd known him, despite coming from a family that loved him. He always had a connection with Alex I never understood, but because I don't have siblings, I couldn't claim to know if it was abnormal or not.*

## TEN

*Jonah had a problem with drugs and never knew when to stop. I liked to smoke the occasional joint but that stopped a long time ago, when my hockey coach informed me I had a real shot at getting a scholarship. Jonah, on the other hand, moved on to harder stuff. His drinking and reckless behavior became out of control, and as much as I loved him and would do anything for him, it was a dangerous path I'd worked hard to stay away from. My family lived that lifestyle, and for some bizarre reason, Jonah liked the way they were and didn't understand why I was the way I was with them. I lived with my uncle but I wasn't a part of his life. I came and went as I pleased, and when I was home I spent all my time in my room. He was rarely there anyway. He spent most of his time with his chosen whore of the month. He always told me my father's weakness was women, but he was a hypocrite because he was addicted to the same poison.*

*Jonah thought my uncle was cool, that the money he had in stacks overrode the way in which he made it. He liked the power my uncle had in this town. Despite Jonah's Dad being the sheriff, he thought my family dealing drugs and whoring out women gave them a type of power he craved. He was young and foolish to think that, but if I'd learned anything from being Jonah's best friend over the years, it was that once he had something in his head it was hard to convince him otherwise.*

*He was his own person, and he didn't bond with people easily. I was his only true friend and I still don't know why he chose to let me in, but he did, and as his best friend I always tried to be a good one and look out for him. I'd often taken the blame for things he did so he wouldn't get in trouble with his father. I'd been his alibi when he slipped out at night without me to do stupid shit. I always felt like I was in his debt because I was in love with his sister and he knew nothing about it. He wouldn't understand or accept us, I knew it from the beginning, so I made Alex keep us a secret, and it troubled her. I couldn't do this anymore, and as soon as school was done I was going to tell Jonah I was in love with Alex and hope he could deal with it, because nothing was going to keep us apart. Jonah wasn't our only obstacle. Alex's parents were not fond of me, or the family I was born into, but she was willing to risk their disapproval and their wrath so I had to man up and risk my friendship with Jonah.*

*I hated how things were with us. I knew he'd been dealing to kids at our school and that the drugs were coming from my family. They had to be because my family wouldn't tolerate someone else dealing on their turf. I know they used him because they couldn't have me. I've never known a family so hell bent on dragging everyone down to their level. You'd think they would be proud that I was getting out and going to make something of my life, but no, not my family. They saw it as a betrayal of the family name. How pathetic. I worried that I couldn't and wouldn't be able to help Jonah, he was in too deep, and every time I'd tried to help him in the past he threw it in my face. I felt like I owed him because of things with Alex. I'd been behind his back when it came to her but you can't fight fate and I didn't want to. I couldn't because my soul gravitated to hers. We revolved around each other; I needed her and she needed me. Nothing made sense if we couldn't be together. I had so much wrong in my life that when she entered my life I knew it was right.*

# TEN

*She was my right. She was ten years old when I first saw her, and although we were only young, something clicked inside of me. I felt home, content even, for the first time in my whole life. People who have a shitty upbringing and get dealt bad cards are used to the bad but not the good, and when something as good and precious as Alex comes into their life, they need to realize it's fate, a gift, something they need to hold onto with both hands. Maybe with something so amazing and good in their life they don't have to repeat the cycle of what came before.*

*I'd seen just about everything bad you could see in life. I thought it was normal, my Dad beating my Mom, but when he eventually killed her, I knew this wasn't how other people lived, and not how I wanted to live.*

*There were kids in my school who didn't have a great home life, but mine seemed to be in the extreme. I owned it though. I was who I was but it didn't define who I could be, and I wanted to be a pro hockey player with Alex by my side.*

*It was hard for me to make friends. I was a lot more mature than my peers but on a team, playing hockey eclipsed all the shit in my home life. I was a part of a brotherhood there. I felt invincible on that ice.*

*I struggled in school; I think it was communication issues. My vocabulary was pretty much grunting in acknowledgment when being spoken to and head nodding to shit I wanted from the dinner menu. It wasn't that I was incapable or behind for my age, it was the simple fact that I wasn't used to being asked my opinion or a question of importance. I also wasn't used to being heard or taken seriously. My family wasn't conventional or sane. It made it hard for me to relate to my peers and make friends. I was pretty much a loner unless I was on the ice with my teammates or with Jonah, and I didn't care. I wasn't raised on love and hugs so I didn't expect it or look for friendships. I looked for a way out, a way I could count on just me and do what I loved doing.*

*Most kids raised with the parents I had would have followed them down the dark path, but when you're not fucked off your face on drugs but watch others lose their identity from them, it's the best form of 'just say no' you can get. The message I got from drug taking is that it scars everyone around you, washes dreams away, and if it doesn't kill you, it keeps you captive in its grip for life, or sends you to prison.*

*One thing about my Dad; he didn't use his own product or keep it on our premises. That being, said he didn't stop my Mom from using it.*

*We lived in a nice house on the outskirts of town, and despite being raided regularly, the cops never found drugs there. It didn't stop them from seizing our shit all the time. I must have been through ten cells and five laptops over a two year period. We got the things back when they didn't have enough evidence to arrest Dad. He was clever and had been raised in the criminal world by his father, whose name muttered was enough to cause fear amongst the dealers and thieves. He eventually got caught for a speeding ticket and just happened to have an underage hooker with him. Caught red-handed, dick out and cum running off her chin and everything. He lasted two weeks in prison before he was murdered by a twenty-year-old who was trying to impress another inmate. He was stabbed just once with a shiv made from a toothbrush. It punctured his heart, and no one rush-*

# TEN

*es to get you help in prison, so he bled out outside his cell. Hard man Moore, offed by a teenager sent in for grand theft auto. My Dad had a lot to prove and recover from when he took over his father's business, but the criminal world was in his blood, he'd been groomed from an early age to take on that world and he did it well. My Mom was his downfall. He was obsessed with her. She was only seventeen when he first met her. She came to my uncle's with my cousin, and my Dad was there sorting some business, and that was it. He claimed her. She dropped out of school and moved in with him, took a liking to his money and power, and before she knew it he'd knocked her up. She couldn't cope with being a parent or a wife. My Dad wasn't the gentlest of creatures and what once was infatuation turned to resentment and hate. His attention didn't stay with her either. He fucked anything in a skirt and would spend days away from home. Mom got high to escape the life she'd ended up in.*

*I spent a lot of my time with my uncles, but they were no better. It's like they didn't have a parenting gene to share between them. Once I reached eleven, I was classed as a man in their eyes.*

*My uncles and cousins didn't mind using drugs and fucking whores in front of me, and encouraging me to do the same. I lost my virginity by being tied to a chair by my cousins, and a whore sucking my dick without permission until it grew, and then getting one of her whore friends to sit on it. She was easily in her thirties and it was my fourteenth birthday. I'd been living with my uncle for eleven months, six days. They clapped and toasted to my manhood, and any guy friend of theirs they told thought it was the best thing ever, but I cried that night once I was alone. For the first time since watching my mother die and my father go to prison with a life sentence, I just cried.*

*I would have disappeared into the darkness, letting the dark side of my blood swallow me into its hue, but soft, nimble fingers stroked over my shoulder and Alex's warm, small body buffed up behind me and she held me while I cried in my bed. That was the first night she managed to climb the big tree up to my window on her own. I'd been coaxing her to climb it for almost a year but I'd always have to help her until now. She always smelled like home- my idea of an ideal home, anyway. The ones you see on TV in those Christmas commercials.*

# CHAPTER TEN

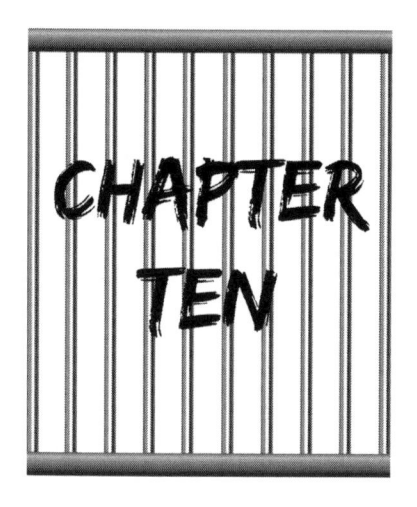

## Dalton

### TEN YEARS AGO

*My bedroom door crashing open drew my attention. Alex stood in the doorframe, her hair messy and sticking up all over the place. Her shirt was ripped from the collar down to beneath her tits, exposing a lilac bra. My eyes scanned over her in slow motion, trying to grab on to reality because this couldn't be it. Her legs were shaking, pulling my attention to the red welts on her inner thigh. Her skirt was higher around her waist than it should have been. My fists clenched, panic rioting inside my chest. I needed to go to her but I couldn't move.*

*I managed to choke out, "Alex? What the hell happened?"*

*Her gaze was unfocused and my feet carried me to her. I snatched her body up into mine, my hands holding her so tight I wasn't sure if either of us were breathing.*

"Jonah's in trouble," she said. I pulled back and scanned her face but she couldn't look me in the eye. "Please help him, Dalton. Please do something. I don't recognize him. He needs help. You have to help him for me… please."

*I pulled back from her, needing the distance.*

"Do you know what you're asking of me?" *I spat, angry that she asked. She knew how hard I'd worked to stay away from that life.*

"I'm frightened." *She quivered.*

"What happened, Alex? Tell me what the hell happened."

*The phone rang and our eyes darted to the receiver. I knew it was him, and no matter what I did to better my life I was dragged into the Moore's world either way. I glanced back at Alex and picked up the phone.*

"Hello?"

"It's Jonah."

"Okay."

*I heard the release of the breath he must have been holding. He'd gotten himself mixed up with my Uncle Keith, dealing for him and sampling way too much of the product and not selling enough. He owed money and was drowning in debt. He needed me to take his stash and offload it, or talk to my uncle about taking it back and leaving Jonah the hell alone. They were playing with fire using him like this with his Dad being the sheriff and all, but it didn't appear to faze them in the slightest. They thought they were above the law and most of my family had done a stretch at one time*

## TEN

*or another; it just meant they were committed to the family way. I fucking hated their fucked up way of thinking. They needed to stop breeding and let the virus of our blood end. Jonah was my best friend and Alex was my life; how could I not help them? I ended the call and made my way back to Alex.*

*"Come and lay down, Alex. Let me get you something to change in to and then you're going to tell me what the fuck happened to you."*

HAD SHE GOTTEN INTO A FIGHT? HAD SOMEONE ATTACKED HER?

*I left her to change in my room and went to open the door Jonah said he was on his way over now before I ended the call with him. He looked like shit. His eyes were bright red, and his hair looked like he'd been pulling it out from the roots; it lay in clumps over his scalp. I hated seeing what he'd become. He handed me a package right there, like he was delivering a cake. I looked around the street, paranoid someone might see him looking shifty as fuck.*

*"Come in," I growled, but he didn't move.*

*"Take it," he pleaded, holding it out to me. I grabbed it from him and widened the door for him to come in, but again, he didn't move. "I know Alex is in there. I know what you did to her," he said in a deep, calm tone, but the shifting of his feet told me he was anything but calm, and I prepared myself for his attack. I always knew the risk to our friendship for loving her, but she was worth every risk.*

*His blow didn't come. Instead he stared at me with a chilling, vacant look in his eyes. Dark silence surrounded us before he eventually turned around and left. I had mixed feelings inside me. I was glad it was out in the open final-*

*ly, but the damage to our friendship may never be fixable. He needed help. He needed my friendship. He was slipping down the rabbit hole and he'd be too far gone soon, and I'd never be able to pull him out.*

*I placed the package in my wardrobe in a shoebox. Pissed was an understatement of how I felt about the amount of product he had given me. What the fuck was my uncle thinking letting an eighteen-year-old kid move this much coke in the first place?*

*There was no way I was risking trying to shift that much product. It would be taken back to my uncle's today, but first I needed to find out what the hell was going on with Alex.*

*I lay beside her on my bed. She'd fallen asleep wrapped in my hoody. I pulled her body against mine and curled my tall frame around her dainty one. I didn't know how long I was out, but I was woken by a loud crash and a flurry of stomping coming up the stairs. My door was kicked open, and armed police flooded into my room, screaming at me to get on the floor. I faintly remember hearing Alex screaming, but it was muffled by the humming in my own ears. I was held down by a knee in my back as my room was turned over, and when the cold pressure of the cable ties tightened over my wrists, I knew. Jonah set me up. Alex set me up. Life as I knew it was over.*

*An arrest for possession with intent to sell a Class A-II is a felony punishable by three to ten years in prison. Jonah had been caught with the entire stash, and they used his fear and his father's influence to play the knock-on effect. If he gave up someone then he would only serve a year. That meant, with his father pulling every string he had, it was in*

# TEN

*a cozy detention center. They had recorded our phone call and had photo evidence of me accepting the drugs - bastards. They kept me for fucking weeks, trying to get me to give up my uncle. Offered me the same deal as Jonah, only I wouldn't have anyone to pull strings for me so I'd end up in the same place as my uncle anyway, and known as a rat. I'd have lasted a day, tops. Either way, my life was over and so was Jonah's, no matter where his Dad got him sent. Ratting on a Moore is unforgiveable, and if you're a Moore, you take the time.*

*So they used me as an example, and because I wouldn't give up my uncle, I got the full ten-year sentence. I was eighteen and tried as an adult, which meant I was being sent to the same federal prison where all the sickest and dirtiest criminals were placed, including my father.*

*My whole being crumbled into dust when the judge read out my sentence, the life I saw for myself dissipated, and if I wasn't so numb I may have cried like a fucking baby. The words of support from my family as I was carted away were what I'd expected from them.*

*"Don't let them break you, boy! See you on the other side."*

*Yeah, thanks a fucking lot. Bye hockey scholarship, and the love that once beat so strong for a girl I couldn't see myself living without turned to stone inside my, cold, frozen chest.*

# CHAPTER ELEVEN

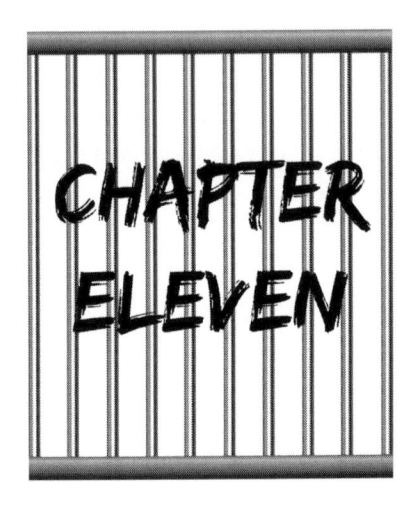

## Alexandria

*Present day*

Every muscle aches. I feel like I've been thrown from a rollercoaster and then trampled by a stampede of elephants. The twin mattress of my old bed didn't help. Pushing back the covers, I assess the scrapes decorating my knees. I didn't even make it into the shower last night. Instead, I shed the spoiled clothes and crawled, naked and fragile, straight under the sheets. Dreams of him haunted me and I kept waking myself with my own sobs.

Wrapping the sheet around myself, I make it to the bathroom to shower, and for the first time, I see myself in the mirror. My hands tighten around the towel and I have to look away.

## TEN

My hair is matted with dried blood from the cut that occurred on the fall inside the bar. My eyes are swollen and blotchy from crying, and the right side of my face is purple. I can't believe this happened to me. I need to erase this whole trip. I need to erase my love, my feelings. I need to erase what we were to cope with what we are now. Nothing.

After scrubbing away the thoughts of last night, I drag myself from the warm heat of the shower and dress in jeans and a tee. I need to focus on the reason I'm home, and that's to pack up Dad's house and make arrangements for his funeral. I didn't tell Mom I was coming, she doesn't even know he's died, but she's on holiday in Rome with her new husband, Rick. She spent years single and pining for Dad, but eventually her heart healed and she moved on. Maybe that will happen for me too.

I begin with my brother's old room. It's like stepping into a time machine. Everything is exactly how he left it. Nothing has been changed or packed away. Clothes lie tossed on the floor, a magazine lies on the end of his unmade bed. There's a musky smell to the room so I open the window and decide that most of this stuff can go straight in the trash. I'll donate to Goodwill the things that are still good.

Memories flicker in front of me like a movie when I find a box of pictures under his bed. My brother wasn't really one for sentiment so it stumps me at first, and then emotions take hold of me and my eyes blur as our teenage years play out in front of me.

*"Get on, Alex. You're coming with us today,"* Jonah informed me, and every nerve ending buzzed with electricity.

*I was allowed to go with them to the watering hole. I was already in my two-piece in anticipation as Dalton had told me the night before he was going to tell Jonah to let me come along today. Jonah had been more laid back lately about me coming places with them, and I didn't question the whys of that. I leapt onto the back of his bike and held his hips.*

*"Where are we going?" I asked, not letting on that I already knew.*

*"I'm taking you swimming. I know how much you love the watering hole and I should take you more, but I've been busy."*

*There was guilt in his tone that I wasn't used to, so I wrapped my arms around his waist and squeezed. "It's okay. Thanks for letting me come," I mumbled into his back.*

*I was getting too big to ride on the back of his bike but the dirt roads we had to take had blind spots so Jonah always felt safer with me on his bike.*

*And from behind him I could watch Dalton without worrying Jonah would catch my lingering gaze. From the first night Dalton kissed me, he found it hard to keep the kisses from happening on a regular basis, and I wasn't complaining. I never felt more alive than when I was with him, locked in a bind of lust. I'd become bolder with him, letting my hands wander to new places on his body, and every time he would groan and then pull away to shower. I was fifteen, and growing more into a woman every day. I liked to tease him by showing more revealing clothes, and when he sneaked through my bedroom window at night to lay with*

## TEN

*me until I fell asleep, I wore the tiniest of shorts. I knew he would be my first and I didn't want to wait, but he did, which almost killed me every time I felt the warm planes of his body against mine. Most girls are scared of losing their virginity, but I wasn't. I couldn't wait to give myself to Dalton, to complete our connection. I was made for him and him alone, so waiting didn't make sense to me.*

*When we arrived, there were others there from our school, including Lisa and Lacy, who both made short time of flouncing over to Jonah and Dalton. They both wore tiny two-pieces that showed off their bodies.*

*"Hey, Alex. It's good to see you outside of school," Lacy said with a genuine smile, and I returned it with one of my own that quickly slipped from my face when Lisa laughed at something Dalton said.*

*"You been dumped babysitting?" Lisa sniggered to Dalton while looking at me.*

*I felt the flush of my cheeks. The last thing I needed was that horrible witch pointing out my youth to everyone. There wasn't even that much of a difference, and as I aged, that difference became less significant.*

*"I don't need a babysitter." I smirked at her and the boys she was with as they approached us. "I'm not a kid anymore."*

*I reached down to the hem of my tee and lifted it from my body, showing off my C cups in a string white bikini I'd bought at the mall after school last week with money Mom had given me for a one-piece.*

*All eyes were on me and I basked in the attention.*

*Yeah, you won't always be able to play the young card,*

*Lisa.*

*I began unbuttoning my shorts when Jonah's hand grasped my wrist. My heart skipped.*

*"What the hell is that?" He snarled, staring at my bikini top.*

*"A swimsuit."*

*"Like fuck, Alex. You don't need to act like these whores to make a statement. You're better than all of them."*

*Lisa's snort at his statement was ignored.*

*"I'm not a baby anymore, Jonah, and I want to wear what the hell I want, not for anyone else, but for me. I like it."*

*I moaned sounding like a baby sister to my own ears.*

*"Do you know how many punks I'm going to have to punch just because you want to flaunt yourself?"*

*God, was I ever going to be allowed to grow up?*

*"I'll keep an eye on her, Jonah. Let her have some fun. It's hot as hell out here and all the girls have on less than her," Dalton said, and caused dragonflies to flutter in my gut.*

*"Fine, but you're keeping the shorts on."*

*I huffed out a puff of air in frustration and shook my head in defeat. "Whatever."*

*I pushed past my brother and waded straight into the water. I felt the ripples move behind me and turned to see Lisa had followed me in.*

*"You might have grown some tits but you'll always be Jonah's baby sister, and no matter how hard you pine for Dalton to see you as a woman, he will always only see that."*

*My eyes misted over at her words. I looked around her to see Dalton and Jonah cracking up over a shared joke. I knew it wasn't true; she didn't know what he and I had, and what we already shared, but the fear from always wondering if we could ever be out in the open tore from the confines I'd buried it in and placed doubt in my mind.*

"You don't know what you're talking about," I snapped, and turned away to try and mask the truth that she'd got to me.

"You know he called me your name once." I stopped moving and tried not to wince from the pain of thinking of him being with her. "At first I was mad but then I found it kinda kinky. I let him pretend I'm you when he comes to me for his fix."

*She's lying.*

"What he doesn't know is I stay in character even when I'm fucking his best friend. I like the taboo feel of it."

I whipped around and splashed water in her face, making her screech like a wild pig being butchered. "You're disgusting, and a lying skank."

"You're a little bitch!" she shouted.

Before she could do anything else, Jonah and Dalton appeared next to us and the whole crowd watched wide-eyed at our little outburst.

"What the fuck did you do?" Jonah growls in her face and her shoulders tense as she flinches from his aggressive stance.

"Nothing. She couldn't take a joke."

I want to tell him what she said but I can't without mentioning the Dalton part.

"Are you okay?" Dalton asks, but I can't look at him right now.

"I'm fine, she just sucks at joke telling," I spat as I walked *past them all to exit the water.*

*The day I'd been looking forward to was nowhere in sight. Instead I just wanted to go home.*

*Jonah followed me out and put a towel around my shoulders. "What did she say to you?"*

*"Have you slept with her?" I asked, and it came out as an accusation.*

*His eyebrows drew together and he shrugged. "Probably. I sleep with a lot of girls, Alex."*

*Probably? Seriously?*

*"You don't know if you've slept with her? What the hell, Jonah? Do you even care that the women you put your dick inside are actual people with feelings? You should at least acknowledge the fact you've slept with them if you have."*

*I didn't know why I was all of a sudden defending Lisa. Well, it wasn't actually her I cared about, but girls like Lacy who really liked him and gave herself to him willingly, hoping it would mean something to him. He couldn't even remember them from one to the next.*

*"What the hell, Alex? I'm stoned half the time and so are they. They shouldn't put out to anyone if they want more from a guy. You're the only girl I'll ever care about. Why do you care, anyway? Has someone touched you like that?"*

*All of a sudden his whole posture stiffened and his pupils expanded. I rested my hands on his shoulders to calm him down and quickly unruffle the feathers I'd riled up.*

*"No, of course not. I just don't like Lisa and I know that she was with Dalton for a while so it's creepy that you share."*

*He shrugged and smiled down at me. "Dalton doesn't care about her or who else is fucking her, he just takes her up on an easy lay when the mood strikes."*

## TEN

*My insides curdled and I was screaming inside while trying to keep myself from bursting out into a full on sob. "Like, still? I didn't think he was still doing that with her," I managed to say, while swallowing the growing lump in my throat.*

*"Sometimes it's just easier to give the chicks what they want so they leave us alone for a bit." He looked over his shoulder at them still in the water in a heated talk. "He's probably knuckle deep in her right now to calm her down."*

*Bile rose up my throat, burning a path into my mouth.*

*"I don't feel good," I whimpered, rushing to find somewhere to compose myself.*

*"Hey, what's going on, Alex? This can't be about not liking Lisa?"*

*"I'm fine. I'm just going to sunbathe for a bit until I feel better."*

I throw the pictures back in the box and stuff the lid back on. I should have been the one kicking Lisa in that alley. She's still the spiteful bitch she's always been, and he was with her after everything. I hate how painful that knowledge is. My head is pounding and I'm starving. I don't really want to leave the house but I'll be damned if I let them make me the victim who hides away. I dust off my clothes and grab my purse.

# CHAPTER TWELVE

## *Never Hurts To Be Nice*

## Alexandria

I'm anxious, I can feel the sweat beading on my forehead and the slight tremor in my hand. Looking around the street before I get out of my car. My wounds are tender and it makes me feel vulnerable. If I see Lisa I want to be prepared for her this time. I'm a grown woman, a parent, and I don't condone violence but I'm also not going to allow her to touch me again without fighting back.

I swallow the uneasy feeling and make my way to the pharmacy.

I grew up here. My Daddy was the sheriff, for Christ's sake.

## TEN

Grabbing some Advil, cotton balls, and antiseptic cream, I ignore the concerned eyes of Mr. Harold behind the counter and don't make eye contact so I'm unapproachable for conversation. Gulping at the air as I exit, I shove the items in my purse and head next door to the bakery to buy some fresh bread and a pastry to eat on the way home. The mixed scent of fresh bread and sugar from the delicious array of cakes in the glass counter causes my stomach to grumble. When I finish eye-feasting on the goods I'm about to buy, my eyes rest on the huge form in front of me. He's extremely tall compared to my 5'5 structure. Tattoos cover all exposed skin and I have to admire the art work; it's intricate, each piece connecting to the next. *Stunning.* The meek girl serving us can't be older than eighteen, and her eyes are wide, but she's playing with her hands as she looks up at the man. He's counting his money out in his hand, asking how much the all-in-one lunch deal is. She informs him it's $4.99 in a quiet tone, and he looks again at the money in his hand before asking for a coffee instead.

I don't know why but I feel bad for him. I'm starving and would hate to only order a coffee knowing how painful my hunger had become, so without thought that I could be offending him, I walk around him and hand the girl a twenty. "I'll buy his lunch deal and one for myself, with a fresh loaf to go, please."

"You don't have to do that." His deep tone penetrates the small space.

I turn, looking up into deep brown eyes surrounded by thick lashes. He looks almost lost - not in the directional sense - but his eyes hold sorrow and loss.

"I'm starving, and there's been many a time I've forgotten my money, so please let me pay for your lunch. It's no problem."

He studies my face, his eyes zoning in on the bruises on my cheek and cut lip. "Maybe I can help you." He nods to my wounds.

"Are you a doctor?" I ask, surprised, and the side of his mouth lifts slightly, forming a half smile.

He's beautiful to look at. I know that's not really a word used for men of his size and appearance, but he is.

"No. I'm referring to the person who inflicted the pain. Maybe I could return the favor?"

My eyes widen and my mouth pops open. I think about that for a moment and smile on the inside before shaking my head. "I just tripped on some trash. I'll be fine."

His brows pinch together as he studies me again before nodding his head in acceptance.

The girl behind the counter hands us our orders and I tell him to enjoy before getting out of there and back to my car to scarf down the hot piece of pie from the lunch menu.

# CHAPTER THIRTEEN

## *Six*

## Dalton

"Ten, there's some guy in the bar asking for you." Jude's voice booms through the closed door to my office.

The fact that he doesn't know the guy asking for me gives me pause. This is a town where everyone knows everyone, especially my family; we make it our business to know.

I smile to myself as I pass Jude and see the swollen eye I gave him yesterday. It wasn't what he did to Alex, it was where he did it. That shit should be reserved for elsewhere. I'm moving too much money through this place to fuck it up by gaining any more attention from the law.

Not that that's a real problem anymore but there are still some officers loyal to Alex's dead father and I refuse to be careless. It pisses me off when idiots behave that way. Jude is my second cousin, and trying to learn the trade, but he's never going to be more than a gopher, running errands. He's quick tempered for one, and loose-lipped for another.

I enter the bar, wary of who I'll find. The images of Alex laying on the floor flare up in my mind, and my eyes scan the floor where I find one of the bartenders cleaning a blood stain that came from Alex's head. As much as I hate myself for it, I haven't stopped thinking about what happened, and if she's left town…

Before I can linger on thoughts of her, a real grin bursts onto my face when I see who's waiting for me. Six! Well, fuck me. His broad frame bumps against mine as he walks over and throws his arms around me, patting me on the back and pulling away as quick as he came in.

"Missed me?"

"You should have told me you were getting out. I would have come to get you, brother!"

He nods, knowing it's the truth. "I had someone to check up on first."

I slam my hand down on the bar, causing Parker, our new waitress, to jump and drop a glass. She might not work out here. She's like a fucking mouse, scared of her own shadow. If she didn't look so good in a skirt I would never have hired her but the locals like the innocent shit she has going on, and getting to stare at her means they spend more time at the bar, spending their money. It's good business.

"Parker, this is Six, and he needs the best bourbon

## TEN

from the top shelf. It's on the house, and don't stop it flowing."

She nods and blushes as she looks at Six, quickly averting her eyes. I'd laugh but that isn't something I ever do. Six is built like a tank, covered in tats with a shaved head that reads, "Vengeance comes to us all" circled round from ear to ear.

He would look scary as fuck if you met him in a dark alley, and rightly so. He harbors a darkness inside him that's thirsty for blood, but to me, he's my brother.

He saved my sanity inside those cell walls. That's where I met him; he's the one who named me Ten, for the ten year sentence I got for someone else's sins. He said it would remind me every day that I was a new person, and that I was owed those ten years. He called himself Six, for the six men he killed, revenging his girlfriend who was gang raped by a rival gang.

I know there's a lot more to his story but he goes to a dark place whenever he speaks about her, and almost becomes a different person, so I refrained from pushing him on details. Everyone is entitled to keep their demons. God knows I keep mine.

He only served time for one of those murders as they didn't have enough evidence to link the others to him, and with gang crime, there aren't many cops looking for answers so evidence gets missed or tampered with. Six went down for second degree murder, which carried a fifteen year sentence without parole. He'd been in five years when I got there. I was his eighth cell mate and the only one he bonded with. It's hard to form real relationships in prison, but when you do, it's for life. Six is like a brother to me and I'd do anything for him.

People who haven't been inside can't understand how it feels to spend one night in prison, let alone years, or even decades.

It makes you different, leaves an imprint on you that's forever binding.

Prison is a lonely place. I woke up every day feeling that loneliness, and it would have defeated me if I didn't have Six.

There's no one to trust, to share your inner chaos with.

It took a long time before I earned Six's trust, and he mine.

Life outside keeps moving forward, but in prison it's about repetitiveness. You wake up for years in the same position on a tiny mattress, at the same time, knowing what's for breakfast because it's the same menu from week to week.

It's the same walls, the same tiny room.

Food is tasteless slop, and the water is warm to drink but cold to shower. You lose everything you considered personal before… crapping in private, showering without having your junk on display, or seeing twenty other cocks in the shower with you.

Nothing is yours. Letters sent to you are opened and read first, calls recorded.

And we were the lucky ones. We were offered some freedom that involved getting to go outside and walk in a circle for half an hour. I could tell you how many cracks there are on the track, or how many times the yard could

## TEN

be lapped within a half hour.

I had to keep my mind from wandering into the dark corners of my head. It's easy to let the depression in, but once you do, it drags you further and further until you can't take it anymore.

The guy in the cell next to ours was twenty-three, and smuggling drugs over the border to earn money for his Mom's hospital bills. He lasted five weeks before they found him hanging from the cot blanket, attached to the bars on his window. They said he went slow and was more than likely hanging there for hours, slowly suffocating. No one should go out like that.

I used my time in there. I gained valuable insights into my father's life and character. I took these insights and applied them to the rest of my family on the outside. I'd never been able to process their mentality. I always felt like I didn't belong with them, but I could teach myself to be one of them. No, not just one of them - I'd run the whole fucking show.

The kid who stepped into this mess would have never thought we'd end up here, but when your life blows up in your face, you either burn to ashes or you rise from them a new person.

These insights allowed me to see what I didn't like about the young man I was before prison. He was a fool for thinking he could escape being a Moore, and for thinking there was light in his dark world. For loving Alexandria Murphy.

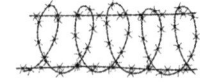

"So I need a place to crash for a while." Six asks dipping his head and shrugging his shoulders appearing almost embarrassed to ask. Well, it's more a statement than a question and he pulls me from my thoughts.

I hate that he got out with no one to pick him up. His Mom died during childbirth. She was a sixteen-year-old runaway, and he went straight into the system and was bounced from place to place until he was fifteen, and he found his own way in life by joining a gang, which became his family. He doesn't talk much about them but I know he left that life when he went to prison and has no desire to go back.

"You have a room with me for however long you need it," I tell him, filling his shot glass and tapping it.

I've been staying in the apartment above the bar, even though I have my uncle's house to go back to if I want to. He's moved in with his latest lay and put the house in my name as requested by my father. Fuck knows why, I hate that place. *It overlooks memories of her.*

"I have a house I'm not using. Come up to my office. I'll get you the keys and Jude can take you there. Tomorrow I'll sort you out a ride."

"I'd like to work. I don't expect handouts."

I smile and slap him on the shoulder. "We can sort that out tomorrow too, but tonight, let's get fucking drunk."

I grab the bottle from the counter and gesture for him to follow me upstairs.

# CHAPTER FOURTEEN

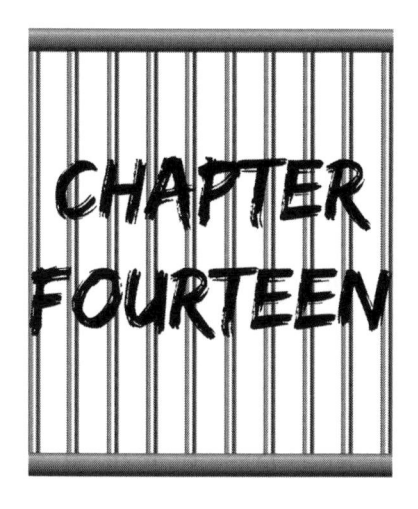

## *Dazed*

## Alexandria

Dry toast sucks! Why didn't I pick up some butter? I miserably gnaw on the toast I made from the fresh loaf I bought yesterday, and sigh at the mess still surrounding me. I made some progress last night and managed to get Jonah's room completely cleared. Just the rest of the house to go. I moan internally, throwing the half eaten toast into the trashcan. I grab my keys and make a run to the store for more trash liners and much needed butter. I feel more tender today then I did yesterday, but used some makeup to cover the mess left on my face. DJ wants to Face time later so I needed to see if the bruise is noticeable with cover up on. It is, but not as bad, and if I wear my hair down I can use that as a barrier as well. Damn, I miss him so much. I'm not used to spending time away from him. Since I was seventeen, all it had ever been was he and I. Mom helped out but she eventually started living her own life.

DJ came as a shock, turning my world upside down, but he was also the saving grace. He helped me survive losing Dalton. I still remember that day and relive it over and over in my nightmares.

*"I'm in trouble." Jonah's dark brows slanted into a frown. His eyes were watery and his jaw trembled as he took a couple of deep breaths before continuing. My stomach dropped with fear for him. "I need you to talk to Dalton. Tell him that if I come to him, he needs to help me."*

*My lips parted in surprise. "Why would he listen to me? You're his best friend; of course he would help you. Tell me what's going on, Jonah. You're scaring me."*

*"I know about you two, Alex. Don't treat me like a fool." His hands reached out and squeezed the tops of my arms in a fierce grip. The skin pinched, causing me to whimper. He was going to find out soon enough anyway, but the pit in my stomach opened up. I didn't want to be alone when he found out. Jonah was so volatile lately, his grip on me was growing fragile, and he knew it.*

*My fear grew with each passing beat of my heart that he didn't speak. I'd planned to make sure Dalton was around when I told him, but now here I was alone with him and he already knew. How long had he known?*

*"I hate it, Alex. I hate that you betrayed me. Both of you fucking betrayed me. He was my best friend. I trusted him,*

## TEN

*and you two have been doing all this shit behind my back."*

*"We love each other, Jonah. We didn't do this to hurt you."*

*I was forced back by his heavy shove, and landed on the bed behind me. "You didn't think about me at all! You were slutting yourself out to him like some Moore whore, and he was lapping it up behind my back, laughing at me."*

*The pain of his words sliced into me. I knew the hurt was alive and vivid in my eyes as water filled them. "I'm not a Moore's whore, Jonah!"*

*I wept and then gasped when his body moved over mine, pinning me beneath him. A shiver of panic swept through me when his hand covered my mouth, and the anger radiating from his intense stare and the strong force of his body kept mine from moving. Looking anxiously towards the bedroom door, willing my parents to come through it, my thoughts turned dark and disturbing when I felt a bulge against the apex of my thighs. Just the thought of it shattered something inside me that would never rebuild. I'd never recover.*

*Please don't let this be happening*

*Who is this person? What's happening?*

*"No, you're not a fucking Moore, you're a Murphy! You want to act like a whore? I'll treat you like one." His tone became emotionless, and it chilled me to the core of my being.*

*The butterfly wallpaper coating every wall pulls me from the hand grabbing at my panties.*

*"Fly away with me," I sang in my mind, as tears soaked my cheeks and my scream was a muted hum against the hard, callous palm covering my mouth. The pain of his knees digging in my thighs as he tried to part them was excruciating. I was five feet two and dainty, and he was a*

*giant in comparison. My mind became hazy as the reality of the situation planted itself like a virus in my heart. My big brother was trying to rape me. How could this be happening?*

*The news I discovered earlier was being washed away with the terror of what was happening in my childhood bed at the hands of my protector. If I closed my eyes and then opened them, would I awake from the nightmare? If I held my breath would I die? Then no one would ever have to know this happened to me.*

*All of a sudden cold air washed over me and the weight holding me down was gone. My body reacted before I realized. I moved, and within a blink of an eye I was huddled into a tight ball, my arms wrapping around my legs as I hugged them against my chest, my chin resting on my knees.*

*"Fuck. Fuck, Alex. I …I'm so sorry," Jonah cried, pulling at tufts of his hair and pacing in front of my bed*

*My body convulsed with tremors I couldn't control. I didn't know why he stopped but the relief that he did brought uncontrollable sobs to tear from inside me.*

*"Don't cry. Damn, I …" He stepped towards me and my hands shot out in front of me to signal him to stop. My head shook from side to side in a frantic motion. "I won't hurt you," he says, bewilderment etched into his features.*

*My breath hitched and my eyes widened, causing the sting from the tears to burn. "You did hurt me, Jonah. Are you crazy?" I screamed, gaining a confidence in my tone that my body lacked in action.*

*"I'm fucked up." He shook his head and a tear leaked from his eye.*

*Despite the hurt, disgust, and fear jumbled inside me,*

## TEN

*my heart weakened when he dropped to the floor and began to cry. Who was this person harboring the body of my brother?*

*"You have to tell Dalton to help me," he sobbed.*

*My mind couldn't cope with the distraught boy in front of me who - minutes ago - tried to sexually assault his baby sister. I searched his eyes anxiously for the meaning behind his words but I knew it was the drugs. He was so freaking high it transformed him into a monster, and if that was the help he needed then Dalton wouldn't be enough to help him. He needed rehab. With my insides still clenched with dread and fear, I bolted for the bedroom door, nearly falling down the stairs as I stumbled down them two at a time. I didn't even close the door behind me as I darted across our lawn and up the steps into Dalton's house.*

I'm startled when I realize I've been sitting in my car but not moving, lost once again in memories of the past. A noise from across the street... *from Dalton's house...* draws my attention. A young woman is giggling as she bounces down the steps. She's definitely doing the walk of shame, only she doesn't look ashamed; not one bit. Her hair is messy and unbrushed, her skirt so short I can see she's pantyless with every step she takes. *Gross.* Make-up is smeared over her face. I slowly graze my eyes up the pathway and steps to the man standing in the doorway. A little bit of me is uncertain whether Dalton will be standing there, and my heart thumps heavily in my chest.

Long, jean-clad legs, narrow hips leading up into a huge torso, defined and painted in artwork. Broad shoulders, thick neck, full lips, and brown intense eyes.

*The guy from the bakery?*

I stare at him for around five minutes before realizing he's gazing straight back at me. I look away, embarrassed, berating myself for acting like a creeper. I'm about to drive away when he steps in front of my car. He places his hands on the hood and stares at me through the window. I'm stunned and don't know what to do, so I get out and shrug my shoulders before raising my hand and saying, "Hi."

*Pathetic.*

"Are you following me?" he asks. His tone is much deeper and more intimidating than the one he used yesterday. He must read the confusion on my face because he stands to his full height and crosses his arms over his chest. "Why were you watching the house?"

I find myself looking over at the house before turning back to him with a frantic shake of my head. "I wasn't. Well, not really. I was going to get some butter and I saw the girl coming out and I was just…" I shrug, flustered. "I live there," I say, pointing to my childhood house. "Well, I don't actually, but I used to. I'm just visiting. Well, not visiting exactly." I stumble over my words, trying to defend myself for being a nosy parker.

"You're adorable."

I look up at him, unsure if I heard him correctly, and he's smiling back at me.

"I was surprised it was you. I was staring like a creep, I'm sorry," I say with a small smile of my own.

"Don't be. You're welcome to stare any time you like." He smirks, and then strides back inside, leaving me standing there rosy-cheeked with embarrassment. *Perfect.*

# TEN

I'm drooling I can feel it. The coffee aroma is driving me insane and they're taking too long making my order. I wonder if they'd mind if I went around the counter and made it myself.

"Sorry about the wait. Tall skinny latte, extra foam." She hands me the cup and I don't have the heart to tell her I didn't want a skinny latte, and I also don't have the willpower to wait for her to correct it. I greedily take the cup and exit. I place the cup to my lips, knowing it's going to be hot and probably burn me, but I'm past caring.

I hit a wall of steel and the coffee tips over my face and drips down my top and into my bra.

"Sugar puffs!" I screech, instead of shouting, "shit" like I wanted to, my mother mouth coming into play for me.

"Haven't you fucking left yet?"

My head rises to see the steel wall is, in fact, Dalton. *Fuck my life.*

I meet his condemning eyes without flinching. *How dare he?*

I respond sharply, with the same anger in my eyes that he holds in his. "Oh, I'm sorry, sheriff of nowhere, I didn't realize that little show the other night was a scare tactic to run me out of town."

He crowds around me and his scent hits me in waves, forcing me to step back and try to not think about how amazing he smells, and how it feels to wake up with that scent on my skin.

"If I wanted to run you out of town, I'd find much

scarier ways to do it than that little run-in you had the other night." His thumb rubs across my mouth, collecting the remnants of my spilled coffee, causing me to gasp from the unexpected contact. He clearly wasn't thinking about what he just did because he snatches his hand away so fast I wonder if I imagined the whole thing.

He's so different to my Dalton; I have to remind myself that he is the same man. *My Dalton doesn't exist anymore.*

"What happened to you?" I find myself asking as my eyes linger on his.

His facade wavers slightly before hardening again. "Is that a fucking joke?"

"We were inseparable once. How can that have changed for you so much?"

His hand grips my chin and I watch as he battles the rage bubbling inside himself. His grasp hurts a little, but not enough to pull away or call out for help.

He keeps me there, unmoving, unspeaking for what feels like forever. Heat and passion flare inside me to mix with my anger as I hold him with the same gaze he has me in.

"Ten."

He releases me and steps away as Lisa saunters over to us. "What's going on?" she asks, accusation clear in her tone. I want to slap her, but instead I push past them both, making sure my shoulder shoves into her. "Watch it, bitch," she screeches at my back.

I turn, straighten up to my not-so-tall height, but enough to warn her that I'm not lying on the floor unsuspecting this time. "Grow up, Lisa, you sure do look like

## TEN

you've aged, you should act it"

    I relish in her mouth dropping open, and turn and leave them to it.

# CHAPTER FIFTEEN

## *Wanting what you can't have*

### Dalton

"I could have made you coffee," Jude says as I walk back into the bar.

He bought one of those coffee machines you put the pods in, but I don't like that fancy shit. I wanted black, strong coffee, and one of those strawberry cookies they sell at the coffee shop. I have a sweet tooth, and those women know how to bake cookies.

I ignore Jude and gesture for Lisa to go straight up to my room.

I look over the order form left on the counter from our supplier and jot my signature on the bottom. My father had everything transferred into my name for when

## TEN

I got out, and let Uncle Keith know I'd be running things from now on. He wasn't happy about it, but he knew he didn't really have a choice; this was his fault anyway. If he hadn't given the drugs to Jonah in the first place, I would have never been sent away. Prison changed me and gave me a lot of time to get to know my father in a way I never had before.

"Ten, are you coming?" Lisa is naked and standing at the top of the stairs, flaunting her flesh to a drooling Jude. She isn't one for modesty, but I was going to fuck her not marry her, so I didn't give a fuck.

I take the steps two at a time and stop her from trying to run back through the door.

"Like to put a show on for Jude, huh?" I tease.

"He doesn't get much action, so no harm in treating him to a little glimpse of what you get every once in a while." She bites her lip. I grab her arm and pull her into me, lifting her and tossing her over my shoulder. "Ten!" she screams, giggling.

I bring her down the stairs and over to the bar where Jude is standing, sorting change for the cash drawer. I put Lisa down on the bar and she yelps from the coldness on her naked skin. I turn her body so she's facing Jude and reach around her waist and part her thighs.

"She wants to give you a show, Jude. What do you think?"

She's wrong about Jude not getting any. He's a dirty bastard and he's had his share of pussy.

"I think it probably tastes as good as it looks." He leans forward and inhales her scent. She grabs his hair and pushes his face against her pussy. He wastes no time diving in, lifting her ass so her back rests on the bar and her head tilts off the edge in a perfect position for me. I unzip my jeans and pull my cock out, tapping her on the cheeks with it before pushing it down her throat. She's writhing and moaning like a nympho, and I have to close my eyes so I can ignore the fact that it's her sucking me off. My mind wanders to the earlier run-in with Alex, and the feel of her lips as I stroked away the coffee. Her words echo in my head. *"We were inseparable once. How can that have changed for you so much?"*

My mind keeps me prisoner and drifts to our first time together.

*I can't look away or deny her. We waited like we promised ourselves we would. I'd been feeling her warm, soft body up against mine for years and never stepped over the line. Kisses and caresses were all I'd allowed us, and it was torture. She was beautiful, always had been. When I stepped towards her and reached for the straps of her summer dress, the air around her crackled with relief. The only emotion on her face was wanting, her teeth pushed into her bottom lip as she nervously bit down. When her eyes clashed with mine, my heart flipped in response.*

*"I'm going to go slow, and if you want to stop at any time, just tell me, okay? We can stop any time. I love you and can wait."*

*"We have been waiting. I can't wait anymore. I need this. I want to be with you completely. I love you." Slowly and seductively her eyes lowered to my jeans, and with a deep breath, she reached forward to un-button them. I caught her hands and smiled down at her, my eyes working*

## TEN

*hard to not roam the creamy expanse of her neck, leading down to the pert, full tits I knew hid just beneath the thin fabric of her bra. "Let's not rush this. You only have your first time once, and I want you to remember and cherish every moment of yours."*

*Her hands dropped to her sides, and sadness lit the amber of her eyes. "Do you cherish yours?"*

*"This will be the first time for me with someone I love. Can this be my first time too?"*

*Her smooth hands slid over the hem of my shirt, lifting it from me and letting it drop to the floor. Her soft palm explored the skin beneath causing a shiver of anticipation to tingle up my spine. I traced my hand down her face and continued to her neck where I could feel her pulse pounding, making my heart stammer in return. I have to fight the overwhelming need to be with her completely so I don't rush one of the most important parts of both our lives. She didn't know how or whom I lost my virginity to, and it was something I'd never tell her, but I couldn't let hers be anything like mine. I needed to make sure she was ready, and felt loved and cherished. Because she was. She was everything to me. I slipped my hands down her arms, taking the straps of her dress with me until it puddled at her feet. Every day my love for her deepened, and in that moment, the intensity of what I felt for her couldn't be measured by anything because nothing compared to the emotion stirring inside me. Her nimble fingers once again found the buttons to my jeans, and this time I let her undo them. I wanted us both naked, bare before each other so we could explore everything we had withheld from for so long. I memorized every inch of her by heart. My soul lit with happiness when I finally en-*

*tered her and she gasped and then smiled up at me. This was life. This was everything. She was everything.*

"Do you want me to come back?"

My eyes open to see Six standing at the end of the bar, completely unfazed by the sex act playing out in front of him. I should have remembered to lock the door. I pull my dick from Lisa's mouth and fasten my jeans. "No. Come upstairs. We can leave Jude to finish this up."

"Ten?" Lisa gasps, but I ignore her. She doesn't have to stay if she doesn't want to, but I've lost interest.

"How was Louisa?" I ask as I sit down at my desk.

Six grins at me and slouches down on the couch in the corner. "A screamer." He nods with a wink.

Louisa was a girl who'd been batting her lashes at me for months, but Lisa kept warning her off. As soon as she saw Six last night, he gained her attention and he ended up taking her home with him.

"I really appreciate the place to crash."

"Don't mention it. Now, you want to talk about work?"

He sits forward, leaning his hands on his knees. "I want to open my own tattoo place. I know that's going to be a problem with licenses and money, but it's something I've always been good at and I just want to do something I enjoy, you know?"

"I can help you with that." And I can. I'm always looking for investments, and I know how talented Six is with a needle.

"Are you serious?" he asks, shaking his head in disbelief.

## TEN

"It won't be expensive to set up, and I have a function room outback that I don't use. It has its own entrance, and with a little money, it could easily be transformed into a studio for you." I lean back in my chair. "It'd be good for business."

There's a knock at the door. I call out for them to come in. Cole and RJ, who work for my uncle, come in. They offer a chin lift to Six and then stand there staring at me. "What?" I ask, annoyed. They look over at Six again like he's an intruder. "He's good. Just say what you have to say."

"Your uncle said he knows a way to get Jonah to come here."

The hairs on the back of my neck prickle and lift. "And that is?"

They look between each other. "Oh, we don't know. He just wants to know if that's what you want."

Fucking idiots. Why didn't he come see me himself, or pick up the goddamn phone? "He knows it's what I want. Do what you have to do."

"Okay." They leave as quickly as they came, and I pull out the bottle of Jack I keep in the top drawer. "You want?" I ask Six, who's staring at me.

"As in *the* Jonah?" he asks.

I pour a shot and shoot it back. "One in the same."

"I'm glad I'll be around." He grins but I can't return it. The whisky is fueling the fire inside my gut. If they get him here, do I have what it takes to kill him? If I don't, I know my uncle will.

# CHAPTER SIXTEEN

## *Missing home*

## Alexandria

It's been a week. I miss DJ like crazy but I won't need to be here for much longer. I grab the last box and take it out to my car. It's the final bits for Goodwill; everything else has been cleared. I saved my own room for last. It was therapeutic getting rid of all the stuff that now feels like a lie. Pictures, gifts, and diaries I'd written from the age of fourteen until I was sixteen. I sat unmoving for a full day when I found the passage of mine and Dalton's first time together, and then finding out I was pregnant. I didn't even get time to tell him. I lost so much on the day he went away. My Dad, Jonah, and *him*.

The bottom of the box I'm holding gives way and the

## TEN

contents spills free. Damn it.

"Hey, let me help you."

I turn to see the guy from the bakery. I guess he's the neighbor now, until I'm finished here, that is. "You were standing there just staring into space." He smiles.

Shrugging, I bend down to help him pick up the contents of the box.

"I was in a different world."

"One better than here?"

A sigh leaves my lips. "No, not really."

His giant palm comes to rest on my shoulder. "Are you okay? You can always come over if you want to talk, or if you need me to help you in any way. Is someone harassing you?" His eyebrows pinch together.

"No, I'm fine, honestly. I just lost my Dad and this is his place. I'm just sorting through everything and it comes with lots of memories."

He's sweet and I have no doubt he would help me if I needed it; I think he's lonely. I've seen the walk of shame happen every day since the first day I saw him living across the street. It's not just women either. I saw a young guy kissing him goodbye on the porch in the early hours of the morning when I couldn't sleep.

"Is this for you?" he asks, pointing to a removal truck.

"Yeah, it's for the furniture to go to Goodwill." I smile.

"Hey, ma'am. What do we take?" a guy asks, jumping from the truck.

"Everything," I tell him, and hand him the keys. "I'll be back in a couple of hours." I close the trunk of my car. "Thanks for helping me out…?"

"Six."

*Six? What's with the number thing?*

"I'm Alex."

"Alex." He repeats my name and shakes his head. "Of course you are."

"What does that mean?"

"Nothing. You have a good day, okay?"

He doesn't wait for an answer. Instead, he turns and jogs back to his house.

---

I pull up at the restaurant and straighten my dress, I haven't seen Dad's deputy in ten years, Jimmy was Dad's best friend and had known us since we were in the womb. He asked me to meet him here when he learned I was in town and I was looking forward to seeing a friendly face.

He welcomes me with a broad smile and a warm hug. He hasn't aged at all in the years I haven't seen him. His light brown hair with flecks of grey scattered through is still thick and long, the laughter lines around his eyes bring the familiarity of knowing him ten years ago. "How are you darling?" He asks holding out a chair for me to sit in. "I've been better." I laugh but it's more with nerves than humor. I feel weird being here, I'm not the same girl that he remembers.

"I'm sorry about your Dad, he was a good man and will be missed."

I swallow down the lump in my throat. "We're holding a service for him tomorrow, we didn't know you were coming here so we went ahead and organized things." He rests his hand on top of mine. "I hope that's ok?" I nod my head and swipe at the tear falling from my eye. "That's lovely, it feels right that you should get your goodbye."

The waitress comes over to take our order and we spend the next two hours talking about Dad and he catches me up on his family. I leave there feeling lighter and almost more at home here.

# CHAPTER SEVENTEEN

*I don't like people*

## Dalton

I'm staring at Lisa who's stomping up and down my office and I'm about to toss her through the goddamn window. I have shit to do and she has become more than a pain in my ass now. Her fucking isn't good enough to put up with her shit. I slam my hand down on the table, startling her. "Shut the fuck up and listen to me. I don't know when or where you got confused about what this is between us, but I fuck you for a warm pussy when I need a release. Nothing more. This…" I point to her in my office, "…is never to happen again. If you come on all clingy and acting like we're more than a casual fuck I will ban you from this place and let my uncle know you're spoiled

## TEN

merchandise."

Her mouth opens in shock. Yeah, she didn't know I know she works for my uncle from time to time to earn extra cash. If you're going to spread your legs anyway, why not earn while doing it? I don't judge her for it, I don't care enough to, but I know she didn't want me to know what she is.

The door opens and my uncle walks in. "Out!" he barks at Lisa, and she scurries away.

"Come in," I say sarcastically.

"This was once my office, boy. Don't forget that."

He sits in the seat opposite mine and puts his feet on the desk. He needs a haircut and a toothbrush. He's one of those fuckers who likes to chew tobacco, and the stains on his teeth make him look like an inbred hillbilly. I don't know how he ever got laid. Maybe that's why he fucks whores - they don't discriminate.

"Who's this Six character?" he asks.

"A friend. Why?"

"Because I want to know why you're involving him in Moore business."

I straighten in my chair and lean forward on the desk, shoving his feet off.

"I'm not involving him in Moore business, but if I were, then that would be up to me."

"He's an outsider, Dalton,"

"Not to me."

"Just because you two cozied up and sucked each other's dicks on the inside, that doesn't mean he can be trusted on the outside."

He's getting real close to getting an ass kicking. I don't

need to defend Six to him. I'd trust Six over any one of these fuckers. They left me to rot, to take the blame and do a decade behind bars. I was eighteen! A whole life planned out and waiting for me, and instead I had to pay the piper for their crimes. All the shit I went through comes flooding in like a tidal wave and I'm back there, lost to my memories.

Entering prison for the first time was nerve-wracking, the blood in my veins solidified, and I thought my muscles were going to freeze up, preventing me from moving. My mind was full of uncertainty. A guard told me that I shouldn't show fear because prisons don't want to put a lamb in with the wolves. *Unless they're corrupt as fuck and he knew I was being thrown to the wolves.*

Certain cellblocks were more dangerous than others. One thing remains the same for a first time prisoner: the process of entering prison is not comfortable in the least. I was subjected to a strip search, which involved having to spread my ass cheeks and squatting for a room full of guys who then looked up there. Wonderful.

After hours of medical tests, screening for illnesses such as HIV and other crap, I was given an identity by the numbers printed on my clothes and a fucking jumpsuit which looked more like old man's pajamas than actual clothes. Everything was stripped from me and I became a statistic, a number, an animal that deserved no decency.

The guards laughed right in front of me, joking with each other by mocking my youth and looks.

"He's going to be eaten alive in here."

"I bet he lasts a month."

## TEN

"I give him a week."

Yeah, that might have worked on me if I cared. I was scared how things would play out for me in there, but I welcomed death if that was how things would go. At least I wouldn't be there and wouldn't feel the hole inside my chest left by Alex. I wouldn't have to live in constant uncertainty and confusion.

In the end it came down to her brother or me. I suppose she didn't love me like I loved her.

Allegiances, "friendships", meant nothing to me anymore. I knew I couldn't trust anyone. If someone was nice to me in there, they more than likely had an agenda.

The daunting reality when they walked me to my cell crept into my soul. This cell would be my home for ten years if I made the full sentence. It was a harrowing feeling. Each step sounded like an alarm in my head, mental images of who my roommate would be ran endlessly through my mind on the short journey. We stopped outside a cell. There were no bars like I thought there would be. Instead, a huge grey steel door with a tiny window stared back at me, the number 106 printed in white. My new address was cell 106. In that moment, an ephemeral touch of sorrow and guilt filtered through me as my student counselor's face appeared in my thoughts. She had helped me so much over the years following my father's arrest and mother's passing. She thought I would never end up there, and did everything she could to make sure that didn't happen, and there I fucking was.

Listening to the clank as the door to my cell was unlocked, my eyes scanned a thin cot pad over a metal bunk bed; they didn't even look big enough in width to be twins. A metal toilet sat in the open in the left corner. I didn't see paper. There was a sink but that was as bleak as the rest of the room. All the home comforts of my bedroom were a distant memory; this would be a rude awakening for me.

My eyes diverted to the man on the top bunk staring at me. He stepped down from the bunk with little effort and stood an inch or two above me. He was covered in tattoos and only wearing a pair of boxer shorts that clung to his junk like saran wrap. I noticed my bunk was missing a pillow yet his had two. Did I ask for it? Would the guards make him give it back?

"Don't be shy, kid. This is your new roomie," one of the guards said with a shove to my back, causing me to stagger forward nearly into the chest of the guy still staring at me. *Perfect.*

I dropped the blanket I was given on the bottom bunk and decided it was flee or fight, and as the clanking of the door locking echoed behind me, there was nowhere to flee. I invoked my inner Moore take-no-shit attitude and nodded up to his bunk.

"Is that my pillow?"

The guy's intense dark eyes squinted as they assessed me, and just when I thought he was the silent, deadly type, he spoke.

"Is it on your cot?"

I wanted to smile. Intimidation, and so early on. Fuck that. I needed a pillow to silently scream in to, otherwise I might end up breaking down in front of people and earning myself a beating or someone's bitch pocket.

"I don't know. Was it?" I asked with a chin lift. The

## TEN

guy was bigger than me in weight and height and he was inside for a reason. I may have been poking a very dangerous bear but I couldn't let him win this or he would try to intimidate me over everything.

"I'm taking it back," I declared, and he grinned at me, not with humor, it was more menacing, like a dare. His eyes darkened as the pupils expanded and his eyebrows dropped, making them look hooded.

"You can try."

If I took it he could come at me and he had a much better advantage, so I tried the way Alex always got my pillow, or blanket, or snacks. She was crafty and I always found it adorable. *Fuck Alex.*

I pointed to the sink behind him and asked, "Is that mine?"

I wasn't sure if he would take the bait as nothing in there was mine but he turned to see what I was referring to, and as he did I was quick to grab the pillow and toss it on my bunk. Childish? Yes, but it worked. He turned back to me and chuckled, a deep, real laugh.

"Damn, you must be as young as you look. You can keep the pillow, you earned it." He laughed before climbing back on to his cot.

I didn't say anything. The whole exchange left me feeling even more unsettled. I climbed under the itchy as shit blanket and burrowed my head into the thin as fuck pillow, and prayed Chuckles up there didn't try to kill me in my sleep.

Six taught me so much, and it was crucial to how my time inside played out. He took me under his wing, and although I always thought he would want something in return, he never did. It took some time before he opened up, but one night after someone tried to attack me in the shower and I had to defend myself, he did.

It was scary, but instincts took over and a raw, new energy inside me burst out - rage. I fought back and won. My insides were screaming so loud I thought I'd break out of my skin and morph into something new, something not human. I huffed and puffed like a raging bull as I stood over him bleeding at my feet his eyes bore into my fiery ones for a couple of intense seconds and then everyone went back to their business like it didn't happen.

"Hide your emotions," Six told me when I got back to our cell. "If you want to look tough, do *not* show fear, anger, happiness, or pain. Feelings are your worst enemy because they reveal your flaws, the weakness inside you bound by emotions."

I lay on my cot, listening, taking in everything he had to offer me.

"Both inmates and guards prey on weakness. Don't give them the opportunity to do so."

"Why are you telling me this?" I had to know his angle. I was warned coming in to not be overly friendly with my cellmates, but to ask some questions if they were approachable.

"Maybe you remind me of someone," he said.

I didn't know how to respond to that. Instead I stayed silent while he carried on talking,

"These cells are filled with manipulative people.

They're the worst of the worst and enjoy head games. If someone can figure out what makes you angry, they can use that knowledge to coax reactions out of you. These men have nothing but time and the boredom that accompanies it. Because we're surrounded by each other 24/7 they have unlimited opportunities to test their scheming skills on you."

Had this happened to him?

"These guys are experts at manipulation and finding the triggers to set you off. They learn them from watching you, studying your reactions. All they have is time and you have to remember not everyone in here is innocent. In fact, most aren't." His bunk groaned from his movements.

Did he know I was innocent? No, he couldn't. Maybe he was just as observant as the men he was talking about. Maybe he *was* one of the men he was talking about.

"Is this your first time in prison?" I asked.

"It feels like I've always been here. I got put away when I was twenty. I'm twenty five now."

I wanted to ask what he was in for but I wasn't sure if that was a done thing in real life. The reality compared to the stuff on TV was such a contrast. I couldn't rely on all those prison movies I watched in my lifetime to get me through this. Before I could decide whether to ask, he continued talking.

"Many have been in prison before and will tell you all kinds of stories. Most people lie about why they're in here and tell you sob stories of their innocence, but is anyone really innocent? Others will layer on what they've done to instill fear. You will have to judge for yourself whether to believe any of the knowledge people give you - including me." His mattress shifts and bulges, causing me to lift my arm up just in case the whole frame gives out.

"Why did you pick the top cot?"

It was a question that had been niggling at me. He was huge. His feet hung over the edge and so did his arm. If he'd rolled off in his sleep that would have been some awakening.

"Because I use common sense. It's harder to shiv someone on the top cot, and I can see everything that's going on below me. You have no clue what I'm doing up here in the darkness of the night."

My brow furrowed. What the hell did that mean, and did I want to know what he was doing in the middle of the night alone on his bunk? Fuck no.

His throaty chuckle rattled the cot. "You need to learn to read people. Try to figure out if people have a reason to lie or mislead you. Some fuckers in here will try to intimidate you or mislead you for the hell of it. Be careful."

"How do I know you won't?"

I had to choose my words carefully. Potentially, anything I said to him, no matter how innocent I thought it was, could have been the opposite. It could have been taken out of context. Did he have a trigger? Would he blow up at me if I asked too many questions? Fuck, I hated this.

"You don't. You can't trust anyone."

*Oh great. That's encouraging.*

He went silent after that and I gathered that was his goodnight.

Over the coming weeks he spoke to me every night,

teaching me something new.

"Avoid conversational topics or your opinions of shit you're asked about, like religion or politics. That shit's not taken lightly in here and you can find yourself with a few holes in your chest if your views differ from those asking you about them."

I didn't even know what my views were on those things. I used to think Alex was sent to me from God, but if that were true was he really God, or was it another raw deal from the devil?

"You already see how a lot of groups are all to do with race in prison. Stay the fuck out of racial issues; you don't want a whole crew of angry fuckers coming at you in the shower. The odds won't play out like they did last time. Inside these walls, inmates in a clique are like pack animals. Your father's influence will only get you so far."

I froze at his words. He knew who my father was?

"You know him?"

"Everyone does. Why do you think that junkie came at you the other week? Your father's down in solitude for attacking that idiot's cellmate."

I wondered where he was. I even got to thinking maybe he was transferred and nobody had told me. It wasn't like I ever visited him.

"Why did he attack him?" I asked.

"I don't know. I just know that your Dad is quite the charmer. He has a new nickname now."

"And that is?"

"Hannibal."

My stomach jolted and I wasn't sure I wanted to know

more.

"He bit the guy's wrist. Chewed through the flesh like a ravenous dog. Tore into the artery before anyone could pry him off."

Silence lay thick between us, and suddenly his head appeared over the cot. His eyes were like black pits in the darkness of the night. It was quite haunting. "Is that the Dad you knew?"

He appeared genuinely intrigued about the answer.

"Dad is not really a title he earned, but the man I knew killed my mother in front of me so…" I didn't add anymore. I'd already told him more than I should have. There he was warning me about over sharing and not letting people know personal shit about me they could use, and two seconds later I was spilling deep stuff.

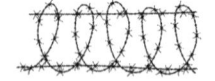

---

Six was the only relationship I had that lasted inside. I got talking to a guy who, like me, was into hockey in a big way. He got sent down for something petty and was told by his homeboys to join a gang when he got inside, because they believed that was the only way to survive inside. The thing about gangs inside is they are far more dominant. They work very differently on the inside than on the outside. My plan was to avoid joining a gang at every cost. Gang members are warriors, and gang leaders demand absolute loyalty. If you were asked to carry out a command it was expected to be done without question. You had no choice, because aside from getting out of prison, there was only one way to quit a prison gang while in prison, and that was by dying.

All prison gangs were separated first and foremost by the races they are typically associated with. Miles, the guy I met, was with the Crips. He was asked to do something he wasn't capable of, and he was killed in a retaliation attack. It felt close, his death. It's not like on the outside when you hear things on the news about shit happening in another state. This is in your space. People came and went, and not always through the front gates. It was hard, and made me even more cautious about not letting myself bond with people. All accept Six.

Six didn't have a clique or crew he hung with, yet he appeared to be respected by them all. Everyone had a chin lift for him when he passed, and some guys even brought stuff to his cell for him. Toothpaste and extra toilet tissue.

In the five years he'd been in there, he must have made a place for himself. Maybe I could do the same.

The most valuable lesson Six taught me was that the normal rules of the outside world simply didn't apply any longer. Prison was a completely different universe. All that mattered was enduring the experience, and surviving until the end with as little damage as possible. And because of him, I did. No one, especially not my uncle who couldn't give two fucks about me, was going to tell me I couldn't trust him.

I didn't have to say anything. Keith knew he lost me to my thoughts so he got up and left.

# CHAPTER EIGHTEEN

## *Enemies*

## Alexandria

I'm so full from dinner. I wish I'd kept one of the beds so I wasn't sitting on a blow up bed that feels freezing beneath me. I dial Leon on Skype, and beam when my baby's face appears on the monitor. "Hey, Mom."

"Hey, baby."

"Leon is in the shower. He wants to talk to you though."

"I will, baby. First tell me about your day."

"I got an A in my Math homework and I signed up for the talent show like you wanted."

"Really? I'm so proud of you."

His cheeks flush with embarrassment and he turns to

# TEN

look at something behind him. "Leon's here now, Mom, so I'm going to take my turn in the shower. Love you."

"Love you too!" I shout to his retreating back.

Leon's face replaces DJ's. "Hello, beautiful. How are things going? We miss you here."

"I know, I'm sorry. I think I was being ambitious trying to sort everything myself."

"You want us to come join you to help out?"

"No," I quickly say. I don't want DJ meeting this version of his father. "I don't want him missing school. That's the whole point of me leaving him with you."

"Okay. I just hate thinking of you going through this on your own."

"I had dinner with my Dad's old friend tonight. He's arranged a service for my Dad, so that's something." I smile, feeling exhausted.

"Alex, do you want to talk about what happened between us?"

Oh God. I'd dreaded him bringing that up. It was a mistake. I love Leon but not in the way he deserves.

"I can see by your face that you don't." He doesn't sound angry. Disappointed, if anything.

"I was wrong for letting that happen." I frown. "I…"

"Don't." He stops me. "Don't say anything else. I want you to think about how good things could be for us if you just gave me a chance to be more than your friend. I love you and DJ, and I think you know that."

"I do. I do, and that's why I trust you with him. I couldn't and wouldn't have asked anyone else to watch him for me. And I love you too, just not in the way you want me to."

"That could change. Just don't say no to the possibility of us."

"Okay," I murmur, feeling defeated.

A knock on the front door startles me.

"I have to go. Kiss my baby for me."

I end the call and slowly approach the front door. Who the hell could that be?

I detach the latch and open the door an inch, not seeing anyone. A breeze carries a strong smell of paint in with it, puzzling me. I close the door to unlatch it and re-open it wide, stepping outside. I can't see anyone, but the smell is stronger. Looking back at the house I pause and my chest begins to pound.

# WHORE

Is painted in red across the front door. What the hell? I spin around, running down the garden, searching for the culprit, angry and hurt someone would do this. It had to be a child, or it could be that freaking Lisa; she's like a child. It would take me forever to wash that off. The cold night air bites at my bare arms and a shiver races through my body. I'm about to turn around and go back inside but I stumble when I see a dark shadow at the side of the house. The person was behind me this whole time and could have gone inside and waited for me because I was stupid enough to leave the door open. He steps into the light of the porch sensor and I recognize him vaguely. Joseph Moore, a second cousin or something along those lines, to Dalton. Did Dalton put him up to this?

"I'm going to call the police!" I shout, hoping he'll be

scared and run away, but he just laughs at me, which chills me, further. I take a step forward and he mimics my action. "You better get the hell out of here!" I shout again.

"Make me."

My hands begin to shake and I have to swallow the lump making its way up my throat.

"You okay over there?" I hear from behind me, and I sigh in relief. I turn to see Six crossing the street. When I turn back the little punk is gone.

"There was someone by my house," I say, and grab Six's arm for support. He looks around at the darkness and then puts an arm around my waist, guiding me inside. "Lock the door. I'm going to check around the house."

I do as he asks, quickly locking the door and checking all the windows are closed.

A knuckle tapping on the door and Six's voice penetrating the wood has me opening the front door for him.

"There's no one there, but I can stay for a while if you want?"

Shaking my head, I thank him for checking for me and assure him I'll be fine and that I'm going to go to sleep and report it in the morning. I can tell by the lines marring his forehead he's not happy, but I just need to sleep these days away until I'm finished here and I can leave this town.

I wake up cold, with an aching back. I feel old for the first time in my life; that stupid mattress offers no support.

A scraping sound coming from outside makes me jump up to open the front door. Six's huge frame blocks the entire entryway. His arms are all sudded up with soap and he's holding a bristle brush. I almost burst into tears at his kindness. "What are you doing?" I whisper.

"I get up early." He shrugged.

"You didn't have to do this."

"I don't like it. It's weak."

I raise a brow, wanting him to elaborate, but he drops the brush in the bucket and walks away. He's right though; this intimidation crap is weak and I'm sick of it. I throw on some clean clothes and grab my car keys.

# CHAPTER NINETEEN

*Mmm Alex*

## Dalton

"**D**alton!"

The hairs on the back of my neck prickle from the sound of Alex's voice carrying down the corridor to my office. What the fuck is she doing here?

The door flies open and her dainty form stands in the doorframe. Her shoulders are stiff, and the brow dipping low as she glares at me almost makes me smile. She was never good at looking pissed at me; her face just couldn't pull it off, there was too much beauty. Maybe that's why I got stung so bad, because I didn't believe she was capable of ugly. *Not all ugly is on the outside.* I should know that better than anyone.

"What the fuck do you want?" I sneer and glare back at her.

"I don't know what the hell your problem is, but tell your family to stay the hell away from me."

Is she serious?

"Are you honestly saying this to me? Ten fucking years, Alex, and you don't know what my problem is?"

"I wrote you and you ignored me." She looks honestly confused; her forehead gains little creases as her eyes dip. Did she really think I would have written her, and written off what she and her family did to me?

"Fuck your letters and get the hell out of my bar before I throw you out."

"Fuck you, Dalton" she spits, and it boils my blood and ignites a fire in my gut.

I storm towards her and she flinches but holds her ground. I crowd her body with mine and lean into her face as I whisper, "You already did fuck me, Alex, and you fucking loved it. Is that why you wrote me? You thought I'd get out and still want to fuck you?"

She pushes at my chest to little effect. "Why would I think you'd want me when you have sluts like Lisa to be your whore and attack dog?"

There's jealousy in her tone, and I'd be lying if I said it didn't please me a little. "Damn. You're jealous of her still? How pathetic you really are."

Her eye twitches and I know I've upset her. Good.

She shakes her head, and her eyes widen and then squint, like she's going to explode. Her tiny fists clench and she blurts out, "You know what's pathetic? Your tiny

## TEN

dick."

She turns to leave but I grab her, pin her front against the frame of the door, and push into her back, making sure my dick rests in the groove of her ass cheeks. I've never been small so her comment is all fumes. I hate that my body still reacts to hers, but it's physical and that's all, and I could use it against her. She fucking owes me.

"Does it feel tiny, Alex? Have you had bigger? Do other men fuck you as good as I did?" I growl.

Her ass pushes against me and her little wisps of breath give away just how desperate she is to be fucked hard and fast. She's panting for it. Poor little bitch probably hasn't had a decent fuck since me. Big headed? Maybe, but I have the junk to back it up.

"They fuck me better than you ever could, Dalton."

I laugh to convince myself the twist in my gut isn't because of the thought of her being fucked by other men. "You were a shit lay, Alex. I only fucked you because you followed me around like a lost puppy all those years and I pitied you."

"Liar." She snarls, trying to push against me, but she only manages to rub herself over my growing cock.

I move my hand up her stomach and her breath catches. Her skin is so soft to touch, my palm heats over the flesh and my dick throbs in response. I carry on travelling up until I cup her tit and squeeze hard enough to make her tense. "I won't lie, your tight, virginal cunt was appealing. I'd never fucked a virgin before. Lisa was good in the sack but someone had been there before me, you know?"

"Fuck you."

"Oh no, but I'll fuck you. I want to hate every inch of

you using every inch of me. "

I rip the cup of her bra down and relish the feel of her hard nipple as it grazes my knuckle. I waste no time grabbing a handful before pinching the hard bud between my fingers.

"Your tits sure did grow. Is this what you came here for, Alex? Because you wanted to cuddle my cock with that tight pussy of yours?" I thrust against her and murmur in her ear. "Is it still tight and warm in there?"

"I came to tell you to sort your family out," she breathes, but it's labored. She's horny as fuck the wanton slut.

"Don't talk to me about my family after what yours did to me."

"What?" she asks, breathless, but way too focused on my other hand that's snaked down the front of her skirt.

"I fucking hate your family. Your mother always turning her nose up at me, yet her son was a fucking loser. Your father acting all high and mighty, wouldn't know honor if it hit him in the face. Your brother, the fucking cunt who knows nothing about loyalty, and you, the little whore who bats her lashes and spreads her thighs to trick men into taking the shit for her family."

"You make no sense. I don't freaking understand anything you're saying. How can you talk ill of the dead? My Dad was a good man."

Is she kidding?

"I was a good man!" I roar. Dropping my hands to her skirt, I hike it up to her waist, exposing her plump ass laced in satin panties.

"But you're not anymore?" she asks.

"Shut the fuck up!" I growl and yank her panties to the side. I pull my cock free from the confines of my jeans and don't bother to push them down my legs.

"I hate you." She sobs, clinging with both hands above her head to the frame of the door.

"I hate you more." I kick her ankles apart to make a big enough gap for me to maneuver my cock between, and then I ram straight inside her. She yelps from my harsh entry and I can't fucking move. Her walls cling to me, choking my dick, and I'm grateful that she's nice and wet for me, otherwise that could have hurt us both.

"How tiny do I feel now, Alex?" I thrust hard into her, jamming her body against the frame. I grab her hips and slide out of her, only to ram back in, pulling her hips back against me. The moans clawing from her throat send me fucking wild. I fuck her hard and fast, watching her ass cheeks slap against my groin, my balls pounding against her clit with every forceful stroke forward. "How much do you hate me, Alex? Enough to let me inside your body, you filthy little slut?"

She's getting off on me being mean to her. Her pussy hugs my cock, flooding it with her juices. I grab a handful of her hair and tug her head backwards so I can see the lust on her face. "Lisa likes to be fucked from behind too. You two have more in common than you think." I grin at her scowl.

"Get the fuck off me!"

I chuckle, pulling out of her and moving away from the heat of her body. She turns and slaps me across the cheek. It stings like a bitch but I don't let her know that, instead I grin at her. I'm not in to hitting women, but I'm not opposed to riling her up.

"You son of bitch" she glares.

I reach forward and wrap my hand around her delicate little neck. "I'm a lot more than that."

Her eyes are still glazed with lust. I drop my eyes to look at her bare, sleek pussy, still with her panties pulled to the side. Her inner thighs are slick with her arousal. I guide her into my office and over to my desk where her ass hits the lip.

"You're soaking for me, Alex, and all your outburst is doing is turning us both on." I drag my finger through her folds, collecting her delicious, wet scent. Lifting my finger to her lips, I trace the outline of her pouting mouth. "You can hate me all you want, but your body doesn't. It wants to be Lisa. It wants to be my little whore."

Her mouth opens and she bites down on my finger. Using the hand that's still around her throat, I tighten my grip in warning. She releases my finger and smirks at me.

"Spread those thighs for me," I say, and smirk back at her when she does so without hesitation. I drop my hand to her pussy and part her folds so I can caress her clit. She gasps when I begin circling the tight bud. Her chest rises and falls in heavy pants, and her hands drop to grip the edge of the table. I look right into her eyes and watch her climb in pleasure. Just as I feel her clit throb, I stop, causing her to shake her head. I bring my hand away and then quickly back down, slapping her pussy and then pinching her clit. She calls out my name and it makes my whole body vibrate. I become frenzied caught up in the sexual need. I circle her clit again until she screams, and then I drop to my knees and suck it into my mouth, flicking my tongue over it. Her hands grab my hair and she's trying to pry my head away, the sensation becoming too much for her. But I fight her, lapping at her pussy like it's coated in the best tasting honey known to man.

"Oh my God, Dalton! Fuck!" she screams, and her pussy convulses around me and gushes her release into my mouth. It's so intense her body shakes and her thighs clamp onto my head, allowing me to burrow into her pussy farther and collect all the fucking nectar I earned from her.

"I need your cock inside me," she begs. I stand and look at her with disgust. I can't let her see how much tasting her after all this time made me feel because I don't want to accept it and won't let her have anything over me.

"Turn the fuck over. I can't come if I have to look at you."

Her face drops and tears build in her eyes. Fuck her tears. I coax her by the shoulders to turn around, and push on her back to flatten her front across the desk. The desk is a little high for her so she has to tiptoe and it makes her toned legs look fucking unbelievable.

I roughly drag her panties half way down her legs and ignore the tremor that rocks through me at the sight of her bare ass and pink swollen pussy peeking out beneath it. Lining up my cock against her entry, I slowly push in, torturing her and myself. "How hard do you like it nowadays, Alex?" I tease.

"Hard!"

I thrust into her and then pull out so I can slap her pussy, making her gasp. I push back in fast and hard, and pump my hips a few times before pulling out and slapping the tender flesh between her legs again. She loves it, and her moans increase with the contact of my palm against her pink, perfect pussy. It's not long before my balls draw tight and warmth grows low in my gut and up my spine. I pull out of her and squirt my cum all over that flawless ass of hers, rubbing my shaft between the cheeks to bring me down from the high.

"Now get the fuck out of my bar," I tell her as I push my dick back inside my jeans and go around the desk to pick up the paperwork I was working on before she arrived.

It takes her a few moments to compose herself but I don't look at her. She rushes from my office so fast it's almost a blur.

And I needed her to go, if I let her, she'll get inside my mind eliciting a craving only being inside her body can sate.

# CHAPTER TWENTY

*Wanting to feel free*

## Alexandria

Sometimes I wish I were that little girl again, because frustration and achy limbs heal faster than the total destruction of your heart.

"Why is there no medicine for heartache?"

"There is. It's called alcohol," Six replies.

"That just emphasizes the sadness. I can't drink him away. I'm stuck in this shitty place that I've been trapped in for ten years."

"You want me to stay?" he asks, and I feel crappy for dumping my baggage on him.

He came over to check on me and I was in the process of hating myself for succumbing to Dalton's taunts. How could I be so freaking foolish? The way he spoke to me. God, I hate myself. I bite into the sandwich I made but spit it out into the bin. Everything is tasteless. I feel empty being here and need to get out of this town as quickly as possible. I'm in mourning for more than just my Dad. I've lost so much more now. My memories are tainted because the boy in them doesn't exist; the father I'd told my son about is no longer the same man. I never wanted to lie to him, but I didn't want him to know the truth either so I told him that his Dad went away and didn't come back. I also told him about all the beautiful parts of Dalton, things now gone forever. Maybe it's a blessing that he ignored my letters refusing to have anything to do with us if this is the kind of man he is.

I feel dirty for enjoying him inside me so much. *I am a whore.*

As soon as this service is over and I have Dad's ashes, I'm getting on the first plane out of here. I'll sell Dad's house as it is and just be grateful that this place is behind me, and maybe I'll be able to finally move on with my life. I've been on hold. Dalton wasn't the only one who got a sentence. I did too and I'm still serving it. It's time for me to set myself free.

"I'm just going to shower and crash," I tell him, and flinch when he looks around the place.

"It's derelict in here, Alex. You shouldn't being staying in here with no furniture."

"It's fine. It won't be for much longer."

## TEN

I hardly slept at all last night. I lay there going over and over the way I let Dalton fuck me like I was… urgh, Lisa. I'll just put this down to stupidity and try and forget it. I make myself as presentable as possible, which is difficult after I gave away the iron and ironing board. Once today is over maybe I'll have some closure.

Or maybe I'll never have that.

---

I hate driving in a pencil skirt - getting in the car is a nightmare. In fact, I hate wearing this entire outfit. If I'd had more time I would have bought something nicer to wear for Dad. I suppose he wouldn't care what I'm wearing, only that I came here to get his ashes to bring him where he belongs. With his family.

I crank up the radio to drown out the loneliness drenching me, and sing along to Adele's *Hello*, but the lyrics make me think of Dalton and tears overflow onto my cheeks. Is there a quota for tears shed over a lost love? Damn, if I bottled them they could hydrate the desert.

Why do I keep doing this to myself? I let myself get pulled back into the love/hate battle with myself and it's exhausting. I feel like my soul is wilting from the hurt and I can't heal. I need to go home and hold my baby, and remember all the good I have in my life. Maybe I should give things a shot with Leon. Urgh, why does that make me not want to go home? Maybe I'll just stay on my own forever and become a nun, or a lesbian that doesn't do the sex stuff. Is that allowed? I'm so wrapped up in my own head that it takes me a few seconds to spot the blue lights flashing in my mirror. Riding in Dad's patrol car flashes in my mind and a smile tilts my lips for the first time in days.

I pull over, hoping they'll pass by and go catch whoever has caused them to blast their siren, but instead they pull in behind me, their wheels kicking up the dirt. It must be because of the plates. It's a rental car and they probably want to know who's come to town, although it's more than likely got around that I'm here now after the bullshit at Numbers. I rummage through my purse for my license and startle when the officer taps the window.

I hit the electric window button and turn down the radio.

My heart sinks in my chest when I see the name of the officer. Moore.

What the hell?

"Step out of the car, ma'am," he says. His tone is lethal, and I would be lying to myself if I denied being scared right now. I look around and see another man with him, only he's not in uniform. It's Keith, Dalton's uncle.

"What was I doing wrong?" I ask without a shake to my voice, despite my body trembling. I'm still tender from the altercation in the bar and the little prank they played at my house. If that's what you can call it.

"Step out of the vehicle. Now."

I look in the mirrors again, hoping for someone to drive by and stop, but dirt road is the only thing that stretches out behind me and before me. I'm five miles from anywhere and took the back road to avoid having to drive past anyone. The gun tapping my window makes me swallow the dry lump forming in my throat.

# TEN

"Step out of the vehicle now!"

I slowly open the door and step out. The cop grabs my arm and I'm spun, my face crushed into the back of my rental car. Mother of hell, that's going to bruise. I just got rid of the last one.

"I'm going to have to check you for weapons. You were being very uncooperative which leads me to believe you're hiding something."

"That's ludicrous."

His hand pushes down on the back of my head, squashing my cheek against the hot metal of the car. "Move and I'll arrest you for assaulting a police officer and resisting arrest."

Tears burn in my eyes. This is so wrong. I have done nothing to deserve this. I don't understand why everyone blames me for Dalton serving time but I know this has something to do with him; it's all connected to him.

Unfamiliar hands roam over my body, causing bile to rise in my throat, and my body tenses. When his hand drops between my thighs and up my skirt, I fidget, my insides screaming at me to flee.

*Where would you go? To the police?*

"I told you to stop moving. Are you nervous about something?" He pins his body to mine.

"You're searching me for no reason, and in an inappropriate manner. I will report you," I say, hoping I sound stronger than I feel.

His harsh, deep laugh sends shivers through my body. Ice floods my veins when his gun taps against my cheek.

"In case you haven't realized it yet, princess, I'm the law in these parts. Your Daddy made that possible, but he's gone now and the deal that was once in place is now void."

What the hell is he talking about? What deal?

"Keith, do you think I'm being inappropriate?"

"I think you're doing your job. This car was driving too fast, and with a broken tail light, and then she began acting shifty and didn't do what was asked of her."

"I wasn't driving too fast and my tail light isn't out," I sob, ashamed that they have me so scared and vulnerable, and I'm completely lost about their cryptic words about my Dad.

The crunch echoes in my ear from Keith smashing something against my car. "Looks like your tail light is out."

"You bastards!"

The cop's weight is gone from my back in a flash, replaced with Keith's. His scent clings to me like poison mist; it's tobacco fused with liquor and it makes me gag. His hand twists in my hair and jerks my head back. His hot breath hits my cheek and with each syllable his spit sprays my skin.

"Bastards? You and your fucking brother are the bastards and it's about time you paid for your disloyalty. You fuck with a Moore you pay at some point, princess. Now tell me where your fuck up of a brother is living these days."

"I did nothing to any of you! And I don't know where Jonah is! Why are you doing this?"

"You. I actually liked you. I thought it was brave to fuck my nephew knowing your Daddy wouldn't allow you anywhere near him. If only he knew his little princess used to sneak in Dalton's window and squeal like a whore being fucked in every orifice. I used to lay awake and stroke my cock to your little cries."

I'm going to throw up in my mouth.

"I'd like to hear that," the officer says.

I would rather die out here than let them defile me.

The sound of a car makes Keith move away from me. I straighten to look in the direction of the car that's now stopped.

"Officer."

"Jimmy."

*Oh, thank God. Don't leave me with them!*

Jimmy's familiar features come into view and I sigh internally.

"What's going on?"

"Police work. The young lady is driving with a broken tail light."

"I'm sure it wasn't intentional." Jimmy looks down to the broken glass and back up at the men. "Looks like this just happened and she's in a hurry to get to her father's service. Maybe you can show some compassion and let her off with a warning. I'll take her from here, and Keith, I'm sure you can get a truck out here to pick the car up. If you're done on your ride along?" Jimmy pushes his jacket open and places his hands on his hips, showing off an impressive firearm and badge.

"We can't have out-of-towners coming in thinking they can break the law and get away with it."

"Well, Tim, she's not an out-of-towner. She was born and raised right here by the man who gave you that badge. The man who was my best friend, and who's service I'm going to be late for."

Tim Moore? I haven't heard of him before but there are so many Moores, it isn't surprising.

My eyes dart to the police badge on Tim's chest. My Dad gave him that badge?

I see the hesitation in Keith's eyes and sigh when he retreats to their vehicle. I stand frozen until the license plate of their patrol car fades into the distance, and then I collapse to the floor and scream. Jimmy's strong, supportive arms wrap around me and guide me to his car.

"Did they hurt you?" he asks in a husky tone full of … what? Regret?

"I don't understand any of this. Nothing makes sense. I feel like I've walked into the twilight zone. Nothing feels real. I can't grasp on to anything because I'm in the dark about what happened."

My eyes are sore from crying and I know I must look horrendous.

"There are some things you should know. I should have told you straight away. I knew the Moore's might pull some shit."

Swiping at my eyes I shift in the seat to semi face him and wait for him to talk.

"Do you know why Dalton Moore went to prison all those years ago?"

"He was dealing for his uncle. That's where Jonah was getting his fix from, but I didn't know at the time. Dalton never told me he was involved with his uncle's business." It was the truth. I had no idea Dalton was involved, and so deep too. He promised me he wasn't like them and that he was going to play hockey and provide a real life for us.

"Your father hid the truth from you, him, and your

mother. He moved you away for your safety and to keep the deceit from you."

"I don't understand. Please just tell me what happened."

He reaches for his badge and swipes his thumb over it. "He was a good man. A fantastic cop. He always stuck by the law and protected our town. Jonah was a troubled kid, always had been, and he tested your father's patience and abilities to be a good policeman. Your father looked the other way or talked people out of pressing charges against Jonah a lot of times."

I didn't realize things had got that bad but I know how far gone Jonah was in the end. He wasn't the brother I knew. Drugs changed everything about him and it had terrified me.

"Jonah got involved with Keith Moore. He was the one caught dealing."

My gasp echoes out into the silence of the car. "No. I was there when they raided Dalton's house. I was there with him."

"Your brother was working with the federal government to turn in Dalton for a lesser sentence. He asked him to take the drugs. It was a really shitty way of doing things, and not something I condone, but it's usually used to bring down higher ranking members of operations like Keith's."

"Jonah wouldn't do that to Dalton. He loved him. He loved me."

Memories of that day flood into me like cement, hardening, and solidifying my blood.

*I know you're with him, Alex.*

"Dalton wouldn't have taken the drugs from him."

*You need to help him. Please, Dalton.*

"He set him up to save himself," I breathe. "And used me to help him."

"Your father pulled every string he had to help Jonah get out of the shit he brought on to himself. It ruined your father." He reaches over and grabs my hand. "Keith is all kinds of dangerous, Alex. We aren't talking about petty criminals here. Your father knew they wouldn't take this lying down so he had to make a deal with Keith."

"What kind of deal?"

"You and your brother were to leave here and not come back, and they weren't allowed to look for you."

"In return?"

"Keith wanted your Dad to bring on a Moore, recruit him, and push him through the ranks."

I shake my head in disbelief. I can't take it all in. It can't be true.

Opening the car door I all but fall from the car and gasp at the air to fill my lungs. I think I'm having a panic attack. I can't breathe.

"Alex, calm down. Get back in the car."

I bat Jimmy's hands away. I can't right now.

"What about protective custody? If my Dad was that worried, why not come with us and put us all in protective custody?"

"He would have had to tell you the truth. You were sixteen and pregnant, Alex. He was going to arrest Dalton for having under age sex with you from before you turned sixteen, and the way he saw it, he was saving Jonah by letting him set Dalton up, just for a different crime than the

## TEN

one he was guilty of."

That isn't the Dad I knew. He would never have done that... would he?

"The under age excuse wouldn't have stuck, Dalton didn't touch me until I was ready, until I was old enough"

Jimmy holds his hands up and shrugs his shoulders. "Your Father was angry and his mind needed to justify what he was going to do to Dalton."

"What about my Mom?"

"You needed her. He knew that and wanted you to start fresh."

"Did my Mom know Dalton was innocent?" I choke out.

He looks at me like he pities me. How can I have been so freaking stupid? She watched me cry myself to sleep for months. She told me it was for the best when he wouldn't return my letters, knowing how much it killed me to have him ignore me and the existence of our child. How could she have held my son knowing what she allowed to happen to his Dad? I can't forgive her for this.

Dalton. Oh God, Dalton.

"I need you to take me somewhere." I look up and plead without saying the words.

"Okay, sure, but we should get to the service."

I hold my hand up to stop him. "I'm not going."

"Alex."

"Please, Jimmy. I can't."

# CHAPTER TWENTY-ONE

*How did we get here?*

## Dalton

I toss the shot back and enjoy the delicious burn of bourbon. I can't get her out of my head. The feel of her body, the scent on her skin, the sounds she makes. It was supposed to make me feel better but it's just fucking with my head. I hate her but my body can't understand that. It wants her. Hate-fucking her didn't do anything but make me crave the feel of her again.

"The contractor is here," Jude says with a chin lift towards the door.

I stand and make my way across the bar. I had it completely remodeled when I took over, making it more appealing to the younger crowd and not just the barflies that end up owing you more than they spend. It was good for business too. The revenue sky rocketed, and it makes washing illegal funds through the books a lot easier. I hate drugs; I don't take them and can't stand that I have a hand in dealing them, but I'd rather be at the top of the castle than the bottom. They wanted me in the family business, well, then I would be, but it wouldn't have ever been taking orders or being my uncle's lackey. I think he secretly wishes I did manage to get out of this town and leave them to their shit. He hates that I'm in charge. I could even take away the truck company I gave him to run if I wanted to. Keith is in charge of getting product moved around. He still plays a big role and has the respect from our customers so it makes sense to use him, to let him keep enough power to make him feel important, but often remind him that I'm the one who has overall power. Even with my father behind bars, his reach is frightening, and Keith knows it and is afraid of going against my father's wishes. When he questioned my friendship with Six, it pissed me off, and I'm going to show him I can do what the hell I like. I'd contacted the contractors as soon as he left the day he bitched me out about Six.

The room out back will be transformed for Six, and if he wants in with the other side of my business then I'll give it to him. I trust him implicitly, but I also want him to have the chance to go as legit as possible. He spent fifteen years behind bars for avenging someone he loved. He deserves this chance and I'm happy I'm in a position to provide it for him.

I shake Matthew's hand and take him through to the back.

"We got your designs via email and I've looked them over and have a team coming in this afternoon to check the structure to see if anything needs amending, but I don't foresee a problem. What time scale are you looking for?" he asks, looking around the space.

"As soon as you can get it started and finished," I tell him. "I don't want it disrupting business, so the faster you can get it done the better."

He nods while continuing to assess the room. "Okay. I'll get everything finalized and a plan in place and let you know from there."

"Sounds good. Just call Jude if you need entry."

I shake his outstretched hand and show him to the door as Six walks in.

"I like her," he blurts out, confusing the shit out of me.

"Who?" Has he met someone already?

"Alex." My stomach flips. "I know she fucked you up, and I'll always be loyal to you, but I didn't know who she was at first."

What the fuck is he talking about? I hold my hand up to stop his tirade. "Six, you're confusing the shit out of me here. How the fuck do you know Alex?" I don't know if I want the answer, or if I'm stable enough to hear it. He's not talking. He's staring at me, making my nerves ricochet through my system. "Six? Have you fucked her?" It comes out so aggressively he squints at me in warning, but fuck that. I don't like the emotion swirling inside me right now.

"No, it's not like that."

"What's not like that?" I need to pace but I'm too fucking tense to move.

"She seems like a good person and I don't like what's

happening to her. It's weak, Ten. If you need to settle a score then do it. Don't toy with her."

"You know what she did to me."

He begins pacing and rubbing his hands over the tattoos on the side of his head. "I know, I know. Fuck. She just got under my skin. I can see how much pain she's in."

"How do you know her?"

"She helped me once. She lives across the street. Well, *squats* would be a better word. That place is empty."

"What do you mean 'toying with her'?" I'm pissed at him. This is the last thing I ever expected out of his mouth. He fucking gave me the nickname Ten to remind myself of the vengeance I deserve, and now what? Pretty Alex bats those fucking lashes at him and he's pussy whipped too? Does he want her? I can't take this.

I don't wait for his answer. I need a drink.

My feet come to a stop as I enter the bar and see a rumpled-looking Alex. Her eyes are rimmed red from tears. She's pointing at Jude.

I really need to lock the door when the bar isn't open.

"Don't you come near me." She's covered in dirt and her shirt is done up wrong. Jude moves and she flinches, grabbing at the purse on her shoulder. "I have a gun and I will fucking shoot you," she warns him, causing him to halt.

"Jude, get out of here," I tell him. He glares at me but doesn't move. "Fuck off, Jude. Now!"

Jude jumps over the bar and shakes his head at me as he passes.

I move towards her but she steps back, shaking her head.

"I need space to breathe. I need you to let me talk and not be this awful version of you, and try to remember the old Dalton. The one who claimed to love me."

Fuck. She's making this hard for me. Anger and betrayal swirl inside me, trying to chase away any hold she once had on me, but my resolve is failing and I'm transported back to the eighteen-year-old boy whose heart is fucking breaking.

I can't look at her. I can't let her back in. I turn but she shouts, "No, you look at me! You see the damage you've created! You don't even care how much you're killing me, do you? You're killing me, Dalton, and for what? I didn't know. I didn't know!"

My heart is beating so fast I think it might rip straight out of my chest. "You told me to help him." I point right at her. She's lying. She knew. She had to know. She asked me to help him.

"I meant getting off the drugs! I thought that was what he wanted. I didn't know," she sobs. "I didn't know how bad things were, or that he was dealing. Oh God." She covers her face for a few seconds and then sniffs, swiping at the tears falling on to her cheeks. "How could you ever think I would ask that of you? You were everything to me. Every damn thing. I loved you from the minute I could breathe, I just didn't know it then. When I first saw you, that was it. I knew I belonged to you. You belonged to me too and I would never have hurt you on purpose. I would never have let you take that kind of hit for Jonah, or for anyone. I loved you more! I would have always chosen you."

"Your whole family fucked me over and ruined my

entire life."

"I didn't know! I thought your uncle got to you. I didn't know."

I don't know what to believe or what to feel. I thought I'd found something untouchable, something special and rare in such a forlorn, empty time in my life, and then it was ripped away and I don't think I will ever recover from it. I can't risk trusting her again, loving her again. *You never stopped loving her.*

I want to scream. I want the ground to shake and the reality to be a different one.

I have to maintain this persona, and in some ways it is who I am now, but what would my family do if they knew that when I'm alone in the dark, I fade back into that boy who learned the hard way that the ones we love betray us, and that the darkness taunts me? The fear instilled inside me from all that time ago still plagues me in the darkness.

What if it's true and she didn't know? What if all that pain was worthless? Can I ever get rid of this hate I've manifested towards her?

"If you're telling the truth then tell me where your brother is." If she says she would have always picked me, now's the time she can prove it.

Her body deflates and she shrugs. "I honestly don't know. I haven't seen him since that day." She swallows and her eyes drop to the floor.

"Why? How is that possible? He would never spend all that time away from you."

# CHAPTER TWENTY-TWO

*Truths hurt*

## Alexandria

"Why? How is that possible? He would never spend all that time away from you."

He doesn't believe me, and telling him what happened that day is something I never wanted to do.

*You're not a fucking Moore, you're a Murphy! You want to act like a whore? I'll treat you like one.*

"Remember when I came to your house that day?"

"Of course I fucking remember that day, Alex. My whole life blew up."

# TEN

He storms over to the bar and pours some liquor into a shot glass then shoots it back, slamming the glass back down and making me flinch. His hand rests on the bar and his head drops.

"You made me change. Do you remember why?"

His head turns to look over his shoulder at me, searching. "You were all messed up. You looked like you'd been pulled through a bush." He straightens and his jaw tics as he pins me to the spot. "What really happened?" His voice is deadly low.

A warm tear seeps from my eye, and before I speak he begins shaking his head. "He didn't," he says, barely above a whisper.

"He attacked me in my room."

His eyes widen and he grabs the glass from the bar and launches it into the bottles lining a shelf. They shatter in a chorus of breaking glass, and fluids spill free.

"He was so high," I murmur, stepping back when his anger turns to me.

"Don't you make excuses for him."

"I'm not," I say, my body trembling. "I've never forgiven him and don't speak to him." He doubles over and pulls at strands of his hair. "He didn't do what you're thinking, Dalton." He looks up at me and his eyes are full of so much pain I almost collapse from the force of it. "He stopped."

"I saw the bruises," he chokes out. "On your thighs. I saw the red marks."

"He stopped, Dalton." I go to him and he grabs me to him. His strong arms wrap around me, pulling my body against the hard, warm planes of his own. He completely absorbs me; I melt into him like hot rain in fresh snow.

The boy from my youth holds me and it's like sucking in clean air after choking on dirt for all this time.

I'm searching for a way back to the place we were before all this happened. Is it possible to get back there, to get back what we lost? Probably not, so I'll just live in these few moments of his embrace.

"This is all fucking messed up. I don't know how we ended up here. I never saw this for us," he says, breaking away from me, and I mourn the loss. He begins pacing the floor. "All this." He gestures around himself. "Was to get even with everyone who wronged me. It was supposed to help me forget you."

"I didn't do anything, Dalton."

"But you did. You loved me and made me love you."

He wasn't being fair. Loving each other was never a choice for us. We are soul mates; it's ingrained in our bones.

"I keep myself busy to forget you, and when I slip, I try to remember what being friends with your brother cost me. What loving you cost me. But every time I still for the briefest of moments, my heart beating heavy in my chest, reminding me no matter how much time passes, no matter what it cost me, I can't make myself stop loving you."

"Do you want to stop?"

"I want the pain of loving you to stop." He beats at his chest. "I want to cut the fucking thing from my chest to stop the pain of every beat, because as long as my heart beats in my chest, I'll never stop wanting you, loving you, hating you."

"Don't hate me," I beg.

## TEN

He stalks across the room and grabs hold of my face, his palms grasping my cheeks. He holds me there, staring into my eyes. So much passes through his eyes. Memories, confusion, hate, anger, lust, love.

He swipes away the tear that drops with the pad of his thumb and then crashes his lips to mine. He's as erratic as a midsummer storm. I'm not sure if he's going to carry on kissing me or push me away, leaving me cold again.

# CHAPTER TWENTY-THREE

*Reality*

## Dalton

I can't think straight. I have information overload, and it hurts worse than when I thought she betrayed me because I've hurt her and treated her like garbage. I let her get hurt by others and I didn't protect her from Jonah when she was mine. I never thought he was a threat to her in that manner. What kind of person tries to rape his own sister? I want to kill him. I don't know if I'd be able to do it, but now it's the only thing I want to do. I didn't even think of anything like that back then. The thought never entered my mind when she came over looking like that. Then again, I never thought he would do what he did to me. Drugs are the fucking devil's juice and it makes me feel sick knowing I supply that shit to people. I let them all win in the end. Jonah for getting me sent away. My Dad and uncles for getting me in the business. Alex's parents for making me think Alex betrayed me. I lost everything, and so did she. Why are families so fucking cruel? What did we ever do but fall in love?

"Don't hate me," she begs, and it's my undoing

We've been robbed of so much time and I don't want to waste anymore. No one has ever come close to her. The outside world can't touch us in this moment, and just for now, I want to pretend. I want to feel.

I push her against the wall, causing her to gasp, and making my dick attack the zipper of my jeans. Her warm, supple body melts into mine with a moan from her lips.

Our lips collide, tongues dueling for control. I want to consume every inch of her, strip her naked and map out every part that makes her whimper. I tear at her shirt, ripping it from her so it falls from her in a flutter, exposing her soft flesh beneath. I didn't take my time exploring her last time, but this time is different.

I tug at the band holding her hair up so it falls in waves around her shoulders. Pushing both hands through it I direct her face away from mine so I can look into her lust-glazed eyes.

"Are you sure you want this?"

Her lips are red and swollen from our frenzied kissing and it makes me want to suck them into my mouth. Her cheeks are flushed; reminding me of how beautiful she looks when she's consumed with lust.

"It's all I've ever wanted."

She trembles, her hands tugging at the hem of my

shirt. That's enough for me. Usually I wouldn't ask a girl if she was sure, but this isn't just some lay, this is Alex. My Alex.

She pulls the tee over my head and her hands stroke over the tattoos painting my skin. I grab her hands in mine and twist her body to pin her front against the wall, holding her hands above her head and enjoying the wiggle of her ass as she squirms and pushes against my crotch.

"Are you aching, Alex?" I groan in her ear, pushing my hard cock against her ass cheeks and grinding against her.

"Yes," she says in an almost cry, her hungry body trying to gain some friction. Kissing along her shoulders and down her spine, I release her hand and drop to my knees behind her, tracing the slender line of her spine with my tongue. I unzip her skirt and let it drop to the floor before gripping her panties and sliding them slowly down her legs; the scent of her arousal causes my mouth to flood with saliva. Damn, I never thought I'd taste her like this again, and I would have lived with only the memories of her scent, which would have almost been cruel. But here I am, centimeters away from the delicious pink flesh of her pussy, and I can't contain myself. Reaching up, I push her back so she flattens her top half against the wall, leaving her full, delectable rump prone and a gap forms between her thighs. I swipe my tongue from her pussy up her ass, making her jolt from the sensation. Stroking my hand over her heated flesh, I lick and taste her like she's my last meal. I devour and savor her all at once. I tease her opening with my fingers and relish the hot feel of her excitement coating my fingers. I stand, pushing them inside her.

Her head tilts back with a groan, and her silky strands of hair pour down my chest like a waterfall. I'm much taller than her so I can lean right over and take her lips with my own as I fuck her with my fingers. I can't take much more, my dick's about to combust inside my jeans.

I pull my fingers from her heat and turn her around. I look into her eyes, telling her I'm sorry, I'm so fucking sorry for thinking she could do that to me. I'd let the hate overrule everything so it clouded rational thinking. It destroyed me, us, her.

She's so fucking beautiful. I love the thick curves to her body; she's a woman and they suit her. Her full tits have a natural weight to them; I just want to be buried beneath them as she rides my cock.

There are some faint marks on her stomach, and it occurs to me that I know nothing about this Alex. Is she married? Are they marks from having a baby? Oh God, is my Alex a mother to someone else's kid? *No.* She came here alone. A husband or boyfriend wouldn't have made her do this on her own, and she certainly wouldn't let me into her body if she were taken.

"You're the most precious thing I've ever set eyes on," I tell her, and mean every fucking word. I want to commit her - naked and flushed - to memory, just in case she decides she can't forgive me and this is the only time I get to have her.

I unbutton my jeans and shove them to the floor. Stepping out of them, I kick my shoes off and reach for her. I lift her so she wraps her legs around my waist then lower her straight onto my waiting cock. We come together like jigsaw pieces.

"Dalton," she murmurs, and she's looking at me like she wants to talk.

I shake my head. "No more talking." I push into her further, eliciting a gasp from her lips. "But you can scream," I tease, dropping to my knees, forcing her body against mine.

Our bodies glow with sweat and it enables her body to glide over mine with ease. Her hard nipples push into me, and it's heaven. I guide her hips with a rough grip - she likes to be loved harder than most. Her lips nibble at mine as our labored breathing echoes around the room. No drug could give you this feeling; sex is the only drug anyone should ever want. She's in my arms, I have her, and it ignites every fiber of my being. Her walls squeeze and caress me as she glides up and down, twisting her hips as she reaches my tip, her hands pulling at my hair. Burrowing my head between her tits, I taste her skin, lapping over her nipple before taking it into my mouth and sucking hard. Her head falls back and her pussy tightens around me so fucking tight she may never release me.

"Dalton, oh God!" she screams, and it's the best sound I've ever heard. I gently rock with her as she comes down and then lay her back so I can cover her body with mine. Picking up the pace again, I thrust into her. Her face contorts with pleasure with every push forward and I know my face mirrors hers. I reach down, hooking her knee over my arm so I can get deeper, and I watch her as she falls deeper into lust beneath me. Her body loose and satisfied, her hips move to match my own. I love the sound of our flesh meeting, and I look down between her thighs to watch as I slide inside her. It's euphoric seeing my cock

## TEN

slick with her juices, pushing into her hot, pink flesh. She takes me all, coating me in her essence. Her arms wrap around my shoulders and she's almost lifted from the floor. I roll onto my back, taking her with me so her body covers mine, and we move in sync, lost in the utopia of this moment together.

# CHAPTER TWENTY-FOUR

## *Waking up alone*

## Alexandria

He carried me upstairs to his bed and made love to me a further two times before exhaustion claimed us both.

I spread my hand across the sheets and I'm greeted with cold, empty space. I sit up to find my clothes on the end of the bed.

*Not a subtle hint, Dalton.*

He's gone? Our moment is gone. My heart sinks. So that's all it was. A fuck.

We hate, we fuck, we pretend, and then we go back to forgetting we love each other and belong to each oth-

# TEN

er. Who are we punishing but ourselves? I can't do this. I can't, I won't survive it. I won't survive him. I always knew it deep down. He holds a power over me more deadly than any other because he makes me die from the inside out. He does damage so intense it weakens my heart and leaves scars marred in blood burned into my soul

It will kill me to walk away but I never realized how strong I am until it was the only thing I could be. DJ needs me to be his mother. He needs me to be home.

I quickly dress and make my way down the stairs. The place is empty. I look at my watch to see it's past eight; it should be open by now. It's eerily quiet but I'm happy I don't have to do the walk of shame in front of everyone, including Jude.

When I get outside I remember I got dropped off here and have no car. I'm only wearing a shirt that has a couple of buttons missing and a skirt, and it's chilly outside now. A light drizzle peppers my skin.

I begin the walk home and berate myself for not wearing flats today. My feet ache because the heels sink in to the newly dampened grass. I don't want to risk walking on the road and being hit by a car. That would be the perfect ending to this trip.

The sound of a car horn nearly makes me fall in a ditch, and my heart picks up pace. For a fleeting moment I'm terrified it's Keith again, but Lacy's car pulls up next to me. The window lowers and she hesitantly smiles at me. "It's raining," she says, like I didn't know. I'm soaked and my shirt is becoming transparent. "You need a ride?"

I stop walking, crossing my arms over my chest. "If

I get attacked in your car, are you going to just let it happen?" I ask, hating myself for being bitchy as soon as the words left my lips.

"I'm sorry, Alex. I've been so mad at myself for what happened. Just let me give you a ride."

I open the door and get in, noticing she's all dressed up. "Are you going out?"

She grins and wiggles her brows up and down. "I'm going in."

"Okay..."

Her laughter is light and it's a nice distraction from the mess that is my life.

"I'm going to Mason's." She winks. "He likes me to fuck him."

Her eyebrows wriggle again and I wrinkle my nose.

"As in ...?" I don't want to assume what I think she's implying.

She nods and bursts into a fit of laughter. "Don't tell him I told you that."

"I promise I won't. I'm going to try and forget I know that."

The rest of the drive is spent making small talk, and I'm glad she drove by so we could make up before I leave.

We pull up, and dread fills me when I see a figure sitting on my porch. I look over to Dalton's old house and see no lights on so Six must be out.

"What the hell does she want?" Lacy asks, posing it as a question but probably not expecting me to answer. "Do you want me to stay?"

"No, go give Mason his treat. I can handle her."

I get out of the car and shut the door then wave to

# TEN

Lacy through the window and make my way down the path towards Lisa.

"You have some nerve."

"Huh. You're one to talk."

"What the hell do you want, Lisa?"

"You gone."

"You really are stupid, aren't you? You think Dalton loves you? That he'll be with you whether I'm here or not? He uses you when he can't have me and always has."

"I will tear your fucking hair out if you keep talking shit, Alex."

I push into her space, our chests almost touching. "I'm not injured and lying on the floor this time, and I will hurt you if I have to."

"We were together before you showed up and tried to ruin everything. I'm having his kid, Alex, so go crawl back under the rock you came from."

Her words hit me like a fist to the chest. I'm winded by them. She knows she's hit me with a critical blow.

"Well, don't worry. I'm leaving tonight." I push past her.

"Good riddance," she calls at my back, but I'm dying and can't turn around.

I fumble with the keys and unlock the door, pushing inside and slamming the door closed. I grab the pillow from the blow up bed in the living room, cover my face with it, and let it have my full meltdown. Screaming into it, I push it tighter and tighter to my face as more anger, hurt, and pain pour from me like a wave crashing against the shore.

Once I calm myself, I drop the pillow to the floor and

ignore the unstable wobble of my legs. Grasping up my belongings, I shove everything into my suitcase and rush for the door. Once I'm outside I remember I left my car on that dirt road, but scanning the street I see it parked a couple of cars up. Jimmy must have had it brought here. I want to cry in relief; I must call him when I get home and let him know I've left, and tell him he can mail my Dad's ashes to my mother.

I load the car and call Leon.

"Hello?"

"Hey, it's me."

"I know who it is, Alex." He laughs and it's good to hear his voice.

"I'm going to catch the next plane out."

"Really?" He sighs. "That's good to hear. We miss you."

"I know. I'm sorry."

"You sound like you've been crying. Are you okay?"

*How did he know that?*

"Yeah, just a tough day. I'll see you both soon. Kiss my boy for me."

"Will do. He's asleep now so you might make it home for when he gets out of school tomorrow. You can surprise him."

"I'd like that. Thanks again, Leon. I don't know what I'd do without you."

"You never have to worry about finding out."

I end the call and start the car.

# CHAPTER TWENTY-FIVE

## *Family issues*

### Dalton

I can't take my eyes from her sleeping form. She drifted into a slumber when I finished making love to her for the third time. I loved getting to know her body again; it was like the first time all over again. We've both changed over the years, and exploring the new curves, blemishes, and little scars that give character to her skin was like nothing I'd felt before. I loved her with everything I was when we were young, but as you age, everything feels more solid, real, breakable.

"Stay with me in this moment, Alex," I whispered to her sleeping form. I didn't want it to end. I didn't want the reality of what I am now to be the real. I didn't think

I could ever be this way. I thought this was over for me. They say time heals, but for me it doesn't. She heals me.

"Are you fucking kidding me with this shit?" Lisa's irritating voice blares into the room.

I leap from the bed buck ass naked and shove her back through the door. "Shut your fucking mouth!" I hiss, looking back into the room to make sure she didn't wake Alex.

"I can't believe you fell into bed with her after everything she did."

"You don't know what the hell you're talking about. I'm so sick of you and my uncle acting like you know anything about what I went through or how it felt. It was me that did that time. It was me who was betrayed by people I trusted. Not you. Not him. Me."

"I'm pregnant," she blurts out, shocking the life from me for about two seconds. I laugh at her. She's beyond desperate and it's embarrassing. "It's yours, Ten."

"Lisa, I always double wrap when I fuck you, and even then I never finish inside your cunt."

Her face reddens and she crosses her arms over her chest. "That's not true, and condoms split all the time."

"Not with us, they don't. Now take your sorry ass and get the fuck out of my place. And, Lisa, if you go near Alex again it won't be my uncle you need to be frightened of."

"I hate her. She ruins everything and always has. What's so freaking special about her? What is she that I'm not?"

I shake my head, pitying her, and I feel like a cunt for ever dipping back into her. I knew she had always had feelings for me, and I was selfish because it was easy to be with her that way.

## TEN

"She's everything."

"I can be your everything," she pleads.

"You can't be her," I tell her honestly, without animosity.

"I never was anything but a gap filler for her, was I?" She looks defeated and I don't want to rub salt in her wounds.

"We had fun but it's over now. You should be with someone who can give you what I can't."

"And what's that?"

"My heart."

I watch her flee down the stairs and it dawns on me that there's no music coming from downstairs. I creep back into my room and pull on a pair of jeans.

The place is empty apart from Jude and Six standing behind the bar.

"I told him not to open." Six speaks before I can ask. He pours me a drink and slides it down the bar. "I thought you deserved the privacy." He nods at me and looks up the stairs. I forgot he was here earlier. Did he see what went down with Alex and me?

"Do we need to finish that talk?" I ask, unsure of what's between him and Alex.

"It's not like that. I just know a good person when I meet one." He looks at me with his dark, penetrating gaze.

My whole body relaxes and I let out a breath of air. The last thing I wanted was to have something come between him and me.

There's a tap at the door and all our eyes look in that direction.

"It's Jimmy."

I nod to Jude to let him in. Jimmy enters with an air of authority, looking me up and down and then turning his attention to Six who looks fucking intimidating standing with his arms crossed, his muscles bulging.

"Do you want to put a shirt on?" Jimmy asks, looking down at my naked torso.

"No," I answer with a hard tone.

Jimmy is not a pushover when it comes to the law. He's a clean cop, and having him in my place makes me nervous. I won't show him that, though.

"I'm not Murphy, kid. I won't look the other way while Moores think they can run this town. I know what happened to you was a really shitty thing. But Alexandria is an innocent girl and I won't stand by while your family intimidate and assault her no matter who they are."

Six moves a few steps towards him and I hold my hand up to tell him it's okay. I don't want him getting worked up and doing something stupid.

"What are you talking about?" I'm genuinely confused. Is he talking about the Jude thing?

"You cousin and uncle pulled her over earlier."

"And?" I growl, already feeling my hackles rise.

"Let's just say they got handsy, and I wouldn't have liked to have arrived any later."

I hear a crunch from beside me. Six has crushed a glass in his hand, which is now bleeding.

"Who's he?" Jimmy asks, nodding at Six.

"No one you need to know. Don't worry about Alex. See yourself out."

I grab Alex's clothes that either Jude or Six has folded

## TEN

and put on a table then run up the stairs two at a time. My uncle needs to learn a lesson. My insides run cold when I think of his hands anywhere near her. Alex is still sound asleep; she hasn't even changed positions. I throw my clothes on and place hers on the bed.

Six is waiting for me when I get back downstairs. I know sexual assault is a trigger for him and don't even have to tell him he can come with me to confront my uncle.

"Jude, stay down here. If Alex comes down, tell her to wait for me." He nods. "Jude!" I shout, gaining his full attention. "You treat her like you would me, do you understand?"

"Yeah."

---

I didn't quite believe it when I got out to find one of us is a police officer. Tim was twenty when I went down, and most of the time he was away at college. I thought he had got out. It gave me hope that I could, so I was disappointed to find him in the thick of the Moore legacy.

I pull into the truck yard and my hands tighten on the wheel as I maneuver it around to the offices at the back.

Six jumps out before me and I worry about him keeping his cool in here. There is always a lot of crew hanging around here and they carry loaded weapons, and have no qualms about using them.

I push the door open and walk straight into my uncle's

office. He's sitting behind his desk with a girl between his legs. She looks young - too fucking young. She pops her head up, slurping her mouth over his cock as she does, and I know I have the same repulsed look on my face Six has.

"Get out!" I snap at her.

These girls make the choice to be here, I learned that years ago. She isn't a prisoner, nor was she forced into the sex trade. They barge their way in for easy money, and sucking old men's cocks makes them feel like they have some supremacy over powerful men. They're wrong, and they eventually learn that the hard way, but she isn't why I'm here.

Six grabs her arm as she walks past, making her gasp and then mold into him. "You see something you like, big boy? I don't come free." She reaches up on her tiptoes and licks his chin.

He forces her away from him. "How old are you?"

"How old do you want me to be? I can be as young as fifteen if that's your flavor." She winks.

"She's legal," my uncle says. "Just." He chuckles.

"Put your fucking dick away," I tell him then turn to the girl. "And you, fuck off."

He must sense by my tone this isn't a social visit. He puts his dick back in his pants and rests his arms on the desk.

"Who's he, your guard dog?" He smirks at Six.

"Do you think I'd need one?"

We both look at Six when he barks, not changing the passive look on his face. It's a warning of just how brutal he can be without thinking or caring about the aftermath.

# TEN

He comes across indifferent but he's anything but.

"What's this about, Dalton? I have shit to do."

"Like what? Going out with Tim to feel up women he pulls over?"

His grin makes me want to stab him in the fucking eye. "Oh, so this is about that piece of skirt."

"I warned you that she and Jonah are mine."

He stands up, pointing at me. "You also gave me the go ahead to get Jonah here."

"What the fuck has that got to do with Alex?"

"Everything! He's her next of kin. If we arrest her or she's injured, the doctor or station will call him."

"So why not just call him and lie?"

"Because he could call her cell and find out it's a lie." He throws himself back into his chair.

Why is Jonah her next of kin if she hasn't seen or spoken to him in years?

"Wait, so what was your plan? To arrest and injure her?" I'm ready to beat the shit out of him.

"Arrest her, but when Jimmy fucking Harvey came to her rescue we had to rework things."

"What does that mean?" He grins, and I fly across the office and grab him by his collar, lifting him from the seat. "What the fuck does that mean?"

"We went with injured." He smirks.

Six walks around the desk and grabs Keith's arm, pinning his hand to the table. He doesn't hesitate before picking up a paperweight and slamming it down on his hand.

"You motherfucker!" Keith shouts.

"What the fuck did you do?" I demand.

"Fuck you, Dalton! Your Dad will hear about this." He

growls and I don't know if he expects me to cower at the threat of my father. I'm not a fucking kid.

Six slams the weight down again and I hear the crunch of Keith's bones. Blood stains the glass ball and sprays on to Six's shirt. The look on Six's face is unsettling. He likes this, inflicting pain, seeing the blood.

"I'm going to kill you, you cunt!" he shouts at Six, but Six just grins at him.

"You can try."

"What did you do?"

"We cut her brakes. It will get him here, Dalton, and that's what you wanted."

I drop him back into his chair and hurry to the door.

"You're fucking dead, you hear me?" he says to Six, clinging to his damaged hand. "You fucking hear me?"

Six stops in his tracks. "You want to write that down for me or something?" He looks at the hand Keith is cradling. "Oh, maybe you need some help." He grabs a pen and scribbles something down on a piece of paper before picking up a stapler, and without flinching, staples it to his own chest. "There. I look forward to it."

"You're dead. I'm going to come for you."

"Good luck with that." Six grins.

My uncle stares at him but I don't have time to stick around. I leave the room and see a couple of my uncle's henchmen waiting outside. I look them in the eye, showing them I'm their boss. They chin lift their acknowledgment then part so Six and I can get past.

I throw the keys to Six and get my phone out. I call the bar and get no answer. What the hell?

"Step on it, Six," I tell him, and sit in my seat, tense

## TEN

as fuck. I'm so glad Alex is at my place and not out in her car. They could have killed her. Cutting her brakes! What realm of insanity are those fuckers living in? This isn't over but I need to get back to see her safe in my bed.

I jump from the car before it comes to a full stop. I race through the door and see Jude isn't there. I sprint up the stairs and barge into my room. My heart shatters when I find it empty, and her clothes gone. I pull my cell from my pocket and dial her number. She doesn't know I checked her LinkedIn profile to see where she lives, and on there she lists her address and phone numbers. I need to warn her about that shit, too.

The phone just rings and rings, and eats at my nerves with every chime.

I bolt down the stairs and out the door, shouting to Six to wait here, and if she comes, to keep her here.

Jumping in my truck, I dial her again and almost swerve into traffic when she answers. "Fuck, Alex. Where are you?"

"How did you get this number?"

"It doesn't matter. Why did you leave?"

She laughs but it's emotionless. "You left, not me. I'm so tired, Dalton. You took me apart to see inside, and marked everything so I wasn't me anymore. I couldn't function without you. Do you know what it's like to sleepwalk through your life? To not feel like you belong anywhere, because all I ever wanted was to be where you were? I'm lost in my own life, my own skin. I don't live. I barely exist. If it wasn't for DJ, I would have faded into obscurity."

*Who the fuck is DJ?*

"I didn't leave you. I came back."

"Why can't you let me love you? Why do you have to hate me?"

"I don't hate you, Alex. I tried, and only ended up hating that I couldn't hate you. That's not how things are now."

"You shut me out. You punished me."

"I was broken, Alex. I couldn't be fixed. You can't fix me. I was so lost. I'm still lost. Do you want to save me? Because I don't think you can."

"No, but I could have been right by your side, loving you while you saved yourself. Or I could have been broken with you."

I hear a horn in the background and fear roots itself inside my chest. "Alex, tell me where you are."

"I'm going home."

"I'm your home. Tell me you're not driving yourself? You-"

"What does that mean?" she asks, interrupting me.

"It means that you belong here with me. I never stopped loving you. How could I stop loving you?"

I pull up to a stop sign and place my head on the steering wheel. "Where are you, Alex? I'm coming to you."

She's crying.

"I'm coming up to Jewels junction."

My head lifts from the steering wheel at the traffic coming in the opposite direction, and my life flashes like cut scenes in a movie as her words cripple me.

*"Why has he turned his lights off? Back off my ass, buddy! Go around!"*

# CHAPTER TWENTY-SIX

*Crash*

## Alexandria

"*I'm your home. Tell me you're not driving yourself? You-*"

"What does that mean?"

"*It means that you belong here with me. I never stopped loving you. How could I stop loving you?*"

I'm soaring, every molecule inside me is alive and humming with possibility. This is what I envisaged in my daydreams. We could be a family, and he can finally meet our son. Dalton still loving me. This is all I wanted and yet I'm terrified and still hurt about everything. Can I trust him? Can I move here after everything? No, I couldn't bring DJ to this family. My boy is too innocent to have this life thrust upon him. Once they have him they'll never let him go and he'll become another one of their victims to manipulate and turn into one of them.

"Where are you, Alex? I'm coming to you."

I notice the guy behind me has turned his lights off and is riding up my ass.

"Why has he turned his lights off? Back off my ass, buddy! Go around!"

Life can change so quickly. In an instant, everything that is becomes everything that was. I know this better than anyone. What I don't know is why fate aspires to keep me and Dalton apart. If we're created as one and spilt into two to find each other once again in a new life, then why the hell is it so hard for us to be allowed to be together?

*All real life-changing love can't be easy, Alex. Because then we wouldn't know how special it is once we have it.*

The car clips me, hitting me with a little nudge that's enough for me to push down on the brakes and try to bring the car under control, but it's like pushing on air. Nothing happens and my world is sent into chaos.

The pull of gravity is like being sucked by a vacuum in every direction. The pain is too much to register. Sickness threatens as my body is thrown forward then halted by my seatbelt jolting me back and winding me. The airbag explodes in my face, busting my nose, and I can feel wetness coating my face which I know is my own blood. Glass shatters and rains down on me like confetti, and my voice is lost to screams that come without permission. DJ's face flashes into my mind. His first cry when they put him on my belly after I struggled to get him into this world. The first time he opened his eyes and really looked at me. His

## TEN

smile, his first words, him waving me off to come here.

When the car finally comes to rest I'm upside down and destruction litters my surroundings. The horn is stuck and blaring, and all I can think about is DJ leaving his guitar too close to the amp, eliciting a loud humming sound. Pain ricochets through every nerve in my body and threatens to steal me to the sleeping world. He can't lose me, I'm all he has. "DJ…DJ."

"Don't move. I've called an ambulance. Oh, God. Baby, don't move, it's going to be okay." Dalton's voice whispers through the broken window.

"DJ…DJ," I murmur as tears mix with the blood I'm losing.

"What's DJ, baby? Is that a person? Who is he?"

Pain slices into me and I can't grasp onto the breath I need so badly.

"He's… our… son"

# Chapter Twenty-Seven

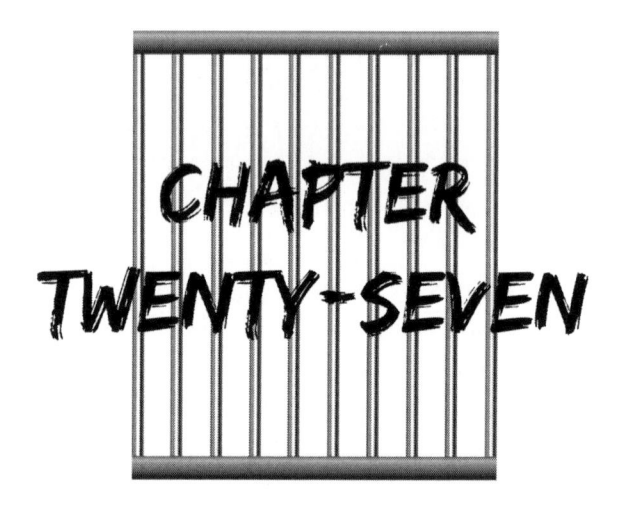

*Broken*

## Dalton

"He's our son," she murmurs through a broken breath before her eyes close.

She's delusional. Brain trauma. Tears build in my eyes and true, undiluted fear washes through me. My hand shakes as I reach in to check her pulse. She can't fucking die on me, I won't allow it. How can this be fair? We were so close to getting the truth we should have always had, and instead I'm given nothing. It's not enough. No amount of time will ever be enough, but I'll be damned if we don't have a least this lifetime together, and die old and decrepit, holding each other in our own bed with beautiful memories of a full life together. Other

# TEN

cars stop and voices hum around me but I can't hear the words. I lie beside the broken car and hold her hand, willing her to be okay. Blue and red lights light up the darkness and I'm being moved away from her. I don't want to let her go. The world spins and nothing feels real. I need something tangible to hold onto but nothing is solid. The world dips and melts away as I watch firefighters begin cutting the car to free Alex from inside. Hopelessness shrouds me as I watch, powerless to save her, to help her in any fucking way.

"What the hell happened, Dalton? Dalton?"

I turn to see Jimmy standing by his patrol car, shouting at me.

"Loving her and her loving me killed her," I whisper, refusing to believe my own words. I drop to my knees and pound the ground beneath me as my mind splinters and my body turns numb.

"She's not dead. Come on, get off the floor. You weigh a freaking ton." I move unconsciously as he guides my body to his car. "We can follow the ambulance."

---

I feel lost. I try to sip the coffee I've been given but I choke. I can't function. I need to breathe her air, see her chest rise and fall, and hear her lips mutter my name.

"Ten." My head lifts to see Six coming at me. "What do you need?"

I'm so fucking grateful to know him, to have him in my corner. I need him now and for what's to come.

"This wasn't an accident. I couldn't stop it happening. I watched her get rammed and when her car flipped I think I died with every rotation."

"Who was driving, your uncle?"

"I don't know, what I do know is my uncle set this up. He cut her brakes, that's enough. He has a vendetta against her brother that needs to be settled, and everyone will suffer until it's done. But it's not his score to fucking settle."

"The Jonah guy that fucked you over and sent you down for ten years is who he wants and will harm everyone until he gets him. It makes me think he was worried about this guy to want him so badly but why now?"

"The drugs came from my uncle so he lost money and I did the time. He had some fucked up agreement with her Dad to get Tim on the force. I knew he was corrupt, doing deals with people who sent me down for a decade, that's its own betrayal, and now the sheriff is dead all bets are off. "

"Motherfucker."

"Alex had nothing to do with it though. I don't think she knows the whole truth about what went down and they moved her out of town before anyone could fill her in. She thinks I just didn't want to see her all this time and then… fuck. The shit I've let happen to her and she didn't have any clue why until yesterday, and then we had each other again. She was in my arms and now she's lying in a fucking surgery room."

His hand comes down to rest on my shoulder, giving it a much needed squeeze, and I need the reassurance that I'm not alone in this, and that someone is on my side and understands my reasons for letting things go down the way they did. I have some serious making up to do and those doctors working on Alex better make sure I get the chance to do it.

"Tell me what you need and it's done." Six nods and the deadly look in his eyes tell me he means he will do anything I need of him. One thing about prison, you're isolated from everyone you once knew and locked in a cage with another person. You either kill each other or you create a bond. Six is a brother to me and if he asked I would do anything for him and vice versa. I need to cash that in now.

"I want the driver, and if we have to go through my uncle to find out who he is, then so be it."

"Okay. I'll let you know what I find out."

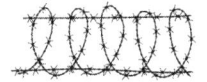

---

Waiting around for an update is slow torture. It's deathly quiet in the small room they have put me in to wait. I'm sure this is the room they take you to when they have to inform you of someone's death. I shake my head to clear that morbid thought. There's another couple in here, and the wife is sniffling into a piece of tissue. It's the only sound and it's coating my body in premature sorrow. It can't end like this.

The door opens and both me and the man with the woman startle and stand. The woman is shaking and can't move.

"Alexandria Murphy?"

My stomach knots and tension stiffens every joint in

my body, making it impossible to move.

I must give him a signal that she's with me without even knowing I have because he comes over to me and pulls off a hair net hat thing.

"Are you her husband?"

"No, a friend. I brought her in."

"Okay, well I have to have the nurse contact her next of kin."

"Doc, I need to know if she's going to be alright."

There's panic in my voice, my tone is low, and there's a slight hiccup when I say *alright*.

Sweat begins to bead on my forehead and I sway slightly on my feet. *Is it hot in here?*

The doctor takes my arm and leads me over to the seat, guiding me down. I don't feel like myself right now. I'm vulnerable and I think I'm in shock.

"The blunt force trauma caused a collapsed lung and bleeding into the chest. We had to go in surgically and repair the damage. She had a severe laceration on the right side of her head from an impact wound that caused swelling to the brain. We're keeping her sedated for now to give her body time to heal itself. She has bruising to the chest and abdomen which was caused by the seat belt. Her nose is broken and she has lacerations from broken glass that will heal with minimal scarring."

I want to fucking cry right now. A grown ass man who hasn't had anything to do with this woman in ten long years, but the love I tried to bury under anger obliterates everything but the strength of my love for her and I came so fucking close to losing her. She's broken right now, and it's because I let my family think they can do what they want. I let them win. After everything I promised myself, everything I promised her, I did the exact opposite. My bar is used for cash drops. I deal the same drugs that got me put away in the first place. I'm a disgrace and I'm disappointed with myself.

"Can I see her?"

"She will be moved to a different room and then you can go in, but not for too long. It should only be family members."

I want to roar that I am her family, that she's the only real family I ever had, but I don't. I tap down the despair and wait.

# CHAPTER TWENTY-EIGHT

*Truths*

## Dalton

Thirty-six hours and she hasn't moved. Not even a flicker - it's torture. I won't leave her side no matter how many times they tell me it's just family who is allowed to stay here. Fuck that. Fuck them. She needs me, she has no one. I wonder about her Mom, and if I should call her, but I don't know if the hospital has already done it. I see Six hovering by the door. He gestures with his head for me to step outside. Squeezing Alex's hand, I untangle my fingers from hers and go to find out what information he has for me.

"You're not going to like this," he warns, but I already knew I wouldn't. Nothing about this is okay. I don't speak and just wait for him to continue.

"They have someone in custody."

"Who?"

"A Lisa Marie." My eyes close briefly, trying to make sense of it all. "It was her car that rammed Alex, and they are accusing her of cutting the brakes beforehand."

This is because I told her I didn't want her.

"I think your uncle more than likely planned for her to take the fall, Dalton. It was Timmy who arrested her and won't let anyone else be there while interviewing her."

I don't need to know how he found out this inside information, I'm just pleased I have him on my side.

"Let her fucking rot." I growl.

"What about your uncle?"

"He will get his," I promise. And he will, I just need to figure out how and when.

"Have you seen Jude?"

"No, nothing."

What the fuck is he up to?

Doctors walk into Alex's room, gaining my full attention. I follow them in, panicking something's wrong with her.

"What are you doing?" I demand.

"We're going to slowly withdraw the medication keeping her asleep so she can wake up on her own."

"How long it will be before she's awake?"

"These things are unpredictable. She suffered substantial injuries, and her body needs time to recover. I know it's not what you want to hear but you have to be patient."

I run my hands through my hair and collapse back into the chair next to her, re-clasping our hands.

"I need you to wake up now, baby. I need you to open your eyes so I can look into them and tell you how fucking sorry I am. This was never supposed to be us. We were supposed to get out and live the dream. All I ever wanted was to run away with you. I wanted just me and you; it's all I ever needed. I've felt like something has been missing inside me for years and I know it's you. You're what's missing. You belong with me. You're in my blood, written in my makeup. You were made to come find me and show me the beauty in the world because all I'd ever seen was the ugly, and I tainted that. I ruined us. I gave away my beauty, my chance, my soul mate because I was angry and hurt and young and fucking stupid. I'll do better, I promise. I'm never going to be perfect, but I promise that every day I'll show you how perfect you are to me."

I swipe at the tears building in my eyes and swallow down the crippling thought that she may not forgive me for everything that's happened and I may lose her.

"Mom," a voice says from the door, and a boy runs into the room and stops at the other side of the bed I'm sitting on. His eyes well up and the tears trickle onto his pale cheeks.

My hand that isn't clinging to Alex is wrapped around the arm of the chair so tight it loses feeling and becomes numb. He looks like me. How is that possible?

A man walks into the room and sighs in relief when he sees the boy, but as soon as his eyes trail up to Alex, he solidifies. I know that look in his eyes. He loves her. Is he

## TEN

with her? Is that boy theirs? Is she married and none of this has been real? No… no it is real. I felt it in her touch, in her eyes, and on her breath when she spoke.

"Who are you?" I ask with a little more venom then he deserves.

His head turns to look at me and then he zones in on my hand entwined with hers. He grabs at the boy, pulling him into him and squeezing his shoulders in a supportive, affectionate manner.

"Who the hell are you?" he replies and it holds the same venom mine did. *Jealousy.*

I release Alex's hand and stand, reaching my hand out. "I'm Dalton. Dalton Moore. Alex and I go way back."

I can tell by the way his eyes expand when I say my name that he already knows that.

"Dalton," the kid says, staring up at me wide-eyed.

"Yeah, that's right, little man. And who might you be?"

"I'm DJ." He nods his head like that should mean something, and it does. It's the name Alex was calling out for; *the name she said belonged to our son.* She did have a head injury; maybe she thought I was this guy, and God, does that drench me in pain. She has a kid with someone else. I was supposed to put babies in her belly, a ring on her finger, and a fucking smile to that beautiful face for the rest of her life.

"DJ," he says again, nodding at me.

"That's a great name, kid."

He smiles up at me and then looks up at the guy yet to introduce himself. He's glaring at me like I'm a piece of shit he stepped in on the way in. I glare right back because I'm a man, and jealous that this asshole even knows Alex, let alone shares shit with her that I don't and maybe never will.

"Mom said you went away and didn't come back," the kid tells me, and I'm shocked that she told him anything about me. "Is she going to be okay? Did you come back because she got hurt?"

I can't talk; I'm frozen, staring at the kid. Why do I feel like I know him? Like I *should* know him.

"How old are you?" I breathe.

The man bends down and whispers something in his ear and then rummages around for change in his pocket, giving it to the kid and gesturing for him to leave. I reach my hand out but I can't speak.

"Does she know you're here?"

He's standing closer to me now and he looks pissed.

"How old is he?" I demand.

He squints, studying me. "Alex never kept that knowledge from you."

"What fucking knowledge?"

A nurse rushes into the room and comes to stand in between us.

"I'm going to have to ask you to leave if you can't keep the volume down," she warns.

I hadn't realized how loud my voice had become but there's one shock after another and I feel like I'm grasping onto something only for it to disintegrate in my hands.

"I'm sorry," I tell the nurse, and reassure her we're good and won't cause any trouble.

The kid comes back into the room and hands me a soda.

"Sorry it's diet. Mom doesn't like me having the full

sugar stuff so I thought she wouldn't want you having it either." He shrugs and shuffles from foot to foot, looking down at the floor.

"How old are you?" I ask, and hold my breath while I wait for his answer.

He looks up and strokes his earlobe. "I'll be ten next month." He smiles at me and my knees buckle. I have to sit back in the chair so I don't fall down. I reach for him and he comes willingly. I take him by the hands and study him. He looks so much like Alex, but like me too. It's overwhelming. He's mine. I have a son? His small hand pulls gently from mine, and as if in slow motion, his hand comes up to my face and swipes so tenderly under my eye, collecting a tear I didn't know had fallen.

"Can I hug you?" I ask, feeling things I never knew existed. It's automatic, the love you have for a child. My mind and soul rearrange everything inside and implant this little life's heart inside my chest, and I never want to live without knowing this feeling. It's magical. We created a life, a son. He's me and Alex all wrapped in a perfect package. His arms reach up around my neck and his little body presses against mine, his head tucking under my chin. I never want to let go of him.

"I'm Leon," the guy still in the room says. "I'm Alex's best friend."

Damn, that's good to hear. I don't want to compete with anyone for her affection but if it comes to it, I will, because there is no way in hell I'm losing her or this boy.

"Her Mom is on her way."

Perfect.

"Police are saying this was intentional?"

I gesture to the door and then release DJ from my arms. "I'm just going to chat with Leon outside for a moment. Can you hold your Mom's hand for me so she knows you're here?"

"Will she know?" he asks, his eyes drooping.

"She will definitely know you're here."

He smiles and hesitantly takes his Mom's hand. I watch him for a few seconds and then follow Leon into the corridor.

He isn't comfortable, it shows in his mannerisms, the way he has his arms folded and the tense jaw.

"What did Alex tell you about me?"

"Only that you went to prison and didn't want anything to do with her." His tone is judgmental and I can't blame him; he has no idea what really happened.

"Well, it's not quite as cut and dry as that. Her brother caused a lot of mess."

His arms drop and his brow furrows. "Wait. Alex has a brother?"

If he's her best friend how can he not know that?

*I haven't spoken to Jonah since that day.*

"How long have you known Alex?"

"Eight years, but she's never mentioned a brother. It's just her and her Mom."

"Are you gay?" I have to fucking ask. I need to know what this is between them, because if he's not gay then how can he just be her best friend? She's beautiful and special; no man could be around her for eight years and not be more, or at least want more.

"What kind of question is that? What the hell does that even matter?"

"Just answer the question." I pin him with a stare and it works.

He shakes his head and lets out an unamused laugh. "No, I'm not gay."

"Do you love her?"

"What?"

"Alex. Do you love her?"

"Yes, of course I do. She's my best friend."

"No. Do you love her?"

There's a silent beat that passes between us despite the hectic noise of people walking up and down the corridor. "Yes, I love her."

"Does she love you?" I have to know no matter if it hurts me. I have to know what I'm up against.

"She's never had room." His eyelids have become heavy with the truth of his words.

"Room for what?"

"Anyone else but you. I thought she would let go and move on eventually, but she never could." He brings his hands up and rubs them down his face. "But I love her enough to just be there for her, and I love DJ and will always be there for him. I don't need to justify or explain myself to you and I'm only telling you this so you know that she hasn't been alone. They've both had someone there who loves them and would do anything for them, and that will always be the case."

As much I want to dislike him, I can't. He has been there looking out for them when I couldn't be. I was so hell bent on hating her, I left her letters unopened and refused her visitation whenever she applied for it. I punished myself by being stubborn and short-sighted. I missed everything.

"I didn't know about DJ, and now that I do I'm going to be a father to him," I warn him so he knows things are different now.

"That's not up to you."

"Like hell it isn't."

"Listen, Dalton, until Alex wakes up and tells me otherwise, DJ will stay in my care. I don't give a shit that you share DNA. All I know is that you didn't want anything to do with either of them. Whether that's changed or not, Alex left DJ in my care."

He walks around me and into Alex's room. A part of me wants to drag him back out and beat him with my caveman stick but I don't want my family knowing about DJ just yet. *If ever.* Especially the way things are at the moment. It wouldn't be safe for him. I'm not safe for him.

"I need to go home to shower and change. I'm going to give you my number and ask that you call me if her condition changes."

He nods but it's not enough.

"I need you to promise me you'll call me."

"I will."

He hands me his cell and I quickly add my number. I look in the room and inhale a deep breath as I look at our son holding his Mom's hand.

# Chapter Twenty-Nine

*Chances*

## Dalton

I push through the doors to the bar and stop when I see Jimmy sitting at the bar with a bottle of Jack. There's no one else here. "Help yourself," I say, pointing to the bottle he's already enjoying.

"We need to talk."

"I need to shower and get back to the hospital." I walk past him to the stairs.

"Did you see him?"

I don't turn around but I stop and wait for him to elaborate.

"Your son."

He has my attention. I join him at the bar and as he's

about to pour himself another drink, I place my hand over the glass.

"You knew?"

"Of course I did. I was her father's best friend. He hated what he did. Who's ear do you think had to listen to his sins?"

"He hated what he did? I don't fucking believe it or give a shit. I still did ten fucking years for his son! He let that happen knowing Alex was carrying my kid."

"He was the father of a sixteen-year-old girl who was pregnant by a Moore."

"I won't let that be an excuse for him, and if that's how he justified his cowardly, selfish actions then I'm glad he's gone so I don't have to pity him for being pathetic."

"The walls are closing in, Dalton. You can suffocate between them or you can get out now while you can."

"What the fuck does that mean?"

He stands and pulls on his jacket. "It means I don't agree with what Murphy did to you. You can be a father, a good man to Alex, or you can go down with your father's empire. I'm giving you a chance to clean the books for this place. It's the only chance I'll give you, and when I come for your uncle I won't go lenient on anyone who is involved with him, including you if you choose the wrong side."

Does he have something on him? Does he know I'm the one running the empire now? No, he couldn't I wasn't stupid, I keep my distance from the product and work from afar to protect myself but the bar's books along with other businesses we own are corrupt as fuck. What if he does have a way of bringing us all down? *Alex.*

## TEN

I can't go back down. I can't. I won't.

The accountant I use for the books is the best there is, and if the books for the bar were subpoenaed they would look legit. But the money in the safe would take some explaining and it takes time to get it through the bar without raising suspicions. We have Swiss offshore accounts and have runs to deliver the funds to those accounts in cash. It's risky to carry that much money but we pay an elite few girls to do all the carrying because they come from there and have family there. They are much less likely to be questioned or have their luggage checked.

"What will you need from me?"

"Nothing. I have someone on the inside. This will be happening soon, Dalton. I'm giving you this chance to get out clean. Don't waste it."

# CHAPTER THIRTY

## *Awake*

## Alexandria

That incessant noise is hurting my head. Why won't someone turn it off? My fingers twitch and I feel someone squeeze them. What the hell is happening?

Spinning and sound of glass shattering around me flashes into my mind. I try to gasp for air and I panic. I was in a car accident.

"She's moving, she's moving!"

I hear DJ's voice and want to cry at the sound. My eyes hurt and feel weighted.

"Alex, baby."

Dalton?

# TEN

"Dalton," I breathe, and regret it when my throat burns. "Water."

"Sure, baby. Here." I feel something at my mouth and I open it to find a straw placed between my lips. I suck and relish the cold fluid as it coats my throat.

My eyes battle to open and when they do, Dalton's face is looking down into mine.

"Damn, it's good to see those eyes of yours."

"How long was I out?"

"A couple of days. Look who's here to see you."

My eyes well when my baby comes into view. I lift my hands, trying to bring him in for a hug, but wires prevent me from full movement.

"I missed you, Mom."

"I missed you too, baby I'm sorry you had to come and rescue me." I stroke the hair back from his face.

"Hey," a familiar voice calls out.

"Leon." I smile. "Come here." He's standing so far away. He walks around the bed to stand by my side, bending down to drop a light peck to my forehead.

"You gave us quite a scare."

"I'm sorry. What happened? Someone was so close. Did they hit me?"

The events are a little foggy.

"That doesn't matter right now. All that matters is you getting better," Dalton tells me, gripping my hand in his. It's surreal seeing both of them together like this, father and son. Does he see how much DJ looks like him? Will he now regret missing out? Nurses walk into the room, distracting me from my thoughts.

They ask everyone to give them space and then speak

to me like they know me, and check the wires going into a feed in my hand. A doctor soon follows and gives me a list of the injuries I came in with, and what they had to do to fix me. I want to curl into a little ball and cry, and the doctor tells me this might happen.

"It's a lot for your mind to cope with. There's a police officer outside who would like to speak to you if you're feeling up to it."

As he says that, Dalton marches from the room and into the corridor. Raised voices follow and then he's back. "They don't need to speak to you. They have all they need."

"What happened, Dalton?" I demand in my feeble voice. I'm tired again already and feel my eyes getting heavy.

"You need to rest," he whispers, walking around the bed to stroke my hair. As my eyes close I see pain on Leon's face. He must be so confused.

---

My eyes open to find my Mom sitting next to my bed.

"Where are DJ and Leon?" I murmur.

"I sent them to go eat. DJ is just a child. He shouldn't see his mother like this."

"Dalton. Where is he?"

She straightens in the chair. "Why would he be here?" Her face scrunches up, showing all the age lines that decorate her skin. She looks old. When did that happen? She's too skinny lately, which doesn't suit her and makes her skin sag a little under her chin.

## TEN

"I know what you did. What Dad and Jonah did to him, Mother." I want to sound more disgusted. I want to be standing so I can poke my finger in her judgmental chest but I think I may break into a crumbled mess on the floor if I try to stand up. I'm physically and mentally worn out. Beaten and fragile.

"What has that boy been feeding you now?" she spits out with her hateful tongue.

"I don't want you here."

"Alex, I flew home from my honeymoon to be here for you."

"I don't care." I try to shout but it hurts the stitches. "Did you even ask Leon what I'm doing here?" I ask, intrigued to know if she bothered to notice where she actually flew back to.

"I assumed it was to do with that hellish boy."

I laugh and then wince in agony. "How can you still keep up this pretense? He did nothing wrong, Mother."

She stands, slamming her handbag down on the foot of my bed. "He was sleeping with an underage teen!"

"I loved him, Mother. I still love him, and you and Dad helped take him away, not just from me, but from DJ."

"He was a bad apple, Alex. Rotten from the seed."

"No, that was your son, not Dalton."

"He is a Moore, Alex. They are all poison."

"My son is a Moore," I remind her.

She huffs an exaggerated breath and turns her back on me. "You're twisting my words."

"Why do you hate them so much?"

Her body swings back around to face me. "What?"

"Why do you harbor such hate for them? What did they do that actually affected you?"

"They got your brother on to drugs. Dalton impregnated my underage daughter," she says in disbelief, like she's talking to an idiot.

"You had this thing about them way before that, Mom, and Jonah made his own bed. He was on drugs way before Dalton was even in the picture and you know it. You just refused to see it because maybe then you'd have to take responsibility."

"You're tired and in pain. You're not thinking clearly. I'm going to go to the hotel and take a nap. I'll be back later to collect DJ from Leon."

"The hell you will."

"What?"

"I don't want him with you. I don't want you here."

"You don't mean that."

"Yes I do."

Snatching up her purse, she flees the room. I buzz for the nurse to tell her I'm in too much pain. I think I busted a stitch.

# Chapter Thirty-One

*Parasite*

## Dalton

I don't know much about girly shit but I know girls like their own things when it comes to clothes and beauty products. Alex's stuff was in the wreck and taken away with the car. I went to the mall and asked the sales assistants to fill bags with everything a woman would need and want. I didn't like the way they looked at me, like I was some sort of hero. I'm not the fucking hero, I'm the reason she's in the hospital. Lisa has issues because of me and it was my family who fucked up Alex's brakes.

I paid with cash and took the bags to the hospital. I hate these places; they have the same cold atmosphere as prison - despair, hopelessness, and pain.

As I get to her floor, my feet halt when I see Mrs. Murphy walking towards me. She is coming straight at me and I don't know how I'm supposed to feel or act. Looking me up and down, she comes to a stop a foot in front of me. She's too fucking close. Her old woman perfume is invading my nose and making me want to sneeze.

Why do all older women wear lavender or vanilla scents?

"You son of a parasite," she spits, surprising the hell out of me. *Son of a parasite?* That's new. "I don't know what you've been filling her head with but it won't work." She pushes one of her skinny fingers into my chest; the tip of her nail bites into the skin. "All you and that uncle of yours do is ruin lives. I won't let Alex be your victim and if you think I'm going to let you near that boy, you have another thing coming."

I've heard enough from her for one lifetime.

"How evil can you be? She's your daughter, and to save your son you sacrificed her happiness. You made your own grandchild grow up fatherless." I shove her finger away.

"He wouldn't have survived prison." She shakes her head.

Is she serious with that bullshit?

"So don't matter about sending an innocent boy to jail instead?"

Her face screws up in a hateful sneer. "Let's not kid ourselves, Dalton Moore. You were not innocent. Alex was sixteen, for God's sake. God knows how long you had her warming your bed. You and your disgusting uncle probably passed her around like candy."

I reach out, grabbing her around the throat, making

## TEN

her drop her purse and pull at my hand. I hear some gasps from people passing us.

"You disgusting old bitch. I loved her and waited until she was ready. I was going to marry her and do right by her. Where do your sick, perverted thoughts come from?" I force her away from me as I release her, and hold my hand up to the security coming my way. "It's fine," I tell them. "She was just leaving."

"How did you get her to come back here?" she chokes out, rubbing at her neck dramatically.

I shake my head in bewilderment. "Her fucking Dad died! How can you not know this?"

She rocks back like I've hit her. "What?"

"Ma'am?" the security man asks. "Are you okay?"

She's too flustered and shocked to answer them. She scrabbles to pick up her purse before she flees. How could she say such things about her own child?

The nurse is with Alex when I get to her room.

"Everything okay?" I ask, concerned that there are some bloody pads in a bowl.

"Just pulled a stitch. She'll be fine."

"My Mom is here." Alex sighs, sounding exhausted.

"I brought you some things." I hold up the bags and place them on the chair beside her bed.

"What's in there?"

"Clothes, underwear, girly shit." I smile and go to stand beside her so I can touch her and breathe her in.

The nurse pulls her gown closed and drags the covers back up her body. "You're all set. Now don't going busting anymore, okay?"

Alex nods and I thank her.

I sit down on the side of the bed and lean over to look in Alex's eyes.

"We have a son." I smile and tears fill her eyes.

"We have a son."

"Leon seems like a good guy."

She shakes her head. "It's not like that."

"But he wants it to be."

"But I don't."

"Why?"

# CHAPTER THIRTY-TWO

## That Boy

## Alexandria

"Why?" he asks, and I'm not going to hide the truth. I'm sick of the lies and secrets. I'm scared to put myself out on display but I'm not hiding anymore. I'm not pretending I can live my life without loving him. It's not possible and never will be.

"Because he isn't you. I couldn't move on. You made me happy in a way no one else ever could. You were always it for me, Dalton, even at ten years old I knew it was you. My soul mate. Why didn't you return my letters?"

Pain flickers in his eyes hearing the sting in my voice. His head comes down and rests on my forehead.

"I didn't read them. I needed to be someone new in there, Alex. You have no fucking idea of what it's like inside those walls. The person I always promised myself, promised you I'd never be, emerged from inside me and took over."

"And who is that?"

"My father. Maybe this was always my fate. You can't escape the sins of the father, right?" He laughs mechanically, standing and throwing his hands into the air and then through his overgrown hair causing it to spike in all directions. His eyes are almost crystallized with the tears threatening to fall. He growls and shakes his head. "I'm not that boy you remember anymore."

"You will always be that boy." I swallow. "And I will always be that girl, missing you. I was haunting myself because a part of me died but couldn't move on when you went away. My light dimmed and I hid it behind fake smiles. I put on my Mom face for our son, so he wouldn't know that I wasn't a whole person because my other half was taken and he never let me come see him. I felt physically weakened by not being near you. I know it doesn't make sense."

"It does. I know exactly what you mean because it's how I felt every fucking day. Only I thought you helped send me away. It was like being dropped in acid and having everything I thought was real stripped and burned away until there was nothing left but scar tissue and a hate so powerful it molded me into someone I didn't recognize. I don't want to be that person."

"Who do you want to be?"

"I want to be someone new. A father. I want to be a

better person for him. For you." He walks back to the bed and grasps my hand. "Will you let me try? I can't lose you again. I can't live without you. Please, Alex. Will you stay even though I've given you every reason not to? Will you love me even when you hate me? Please will you choose me?"

"I would have always picked you, Dalton. People like us, who are meant to be together, always find a way back to each other, even if we have to take detours to get there. Never let me go again," I beg him, grabbing at him to pull him against me. "Promise me you won't leave me again."

"Never. I promise. I fucking promise."

# CHAPTER THIRTY-THREE

*Tender*

## Alexandria

It's been a week. I'm feeling a lot better but still tender. The bruises are bold and ugly. I can't stand seeing myself in the mirror so I avoid them. Leon wants to know what my plan is when I'm released later today and I honestly don't know what to tell him. Dalton and I haven't really discussed our future, and he has the bar and Six here. I don't want my son here with his uncle but I don't want to leave without Dalton either. I need time to fully recover and get my head in the right place. DJ has school; I need to go home. Mom didn't come back after the day I told her I didn't want her here, and I'm pleased, but a part of me is disappointed that she gave up so easily, that she

# TEN

didn't even apologize.

Dalton informed me that it was Lisa who ran me off the road, and that the police are holding her for attempted murder. They said she cut my brakes beforehand, but Dalton was honest with me and told me it was his psychotic uncle. My Mom had filled out all my insurance forms back when I had DJ, and on them she put Jonah as my next of kin instead of her. I won't get to ask her why, but Keith thought Jonah would be contacted and come here if he thought I was hurt. He was wrong.

I fear for Jonah. Keith has his own addiction that involves getting even with our family, and that means getting to Jonah. I hate that he's so hell bent on causing all this crap after ten years. My Dad died, and according to Keith, that marked the end of any deal he made with him. I'll never be safe here and neither will DJ. Dalton knows this and keeps telling me that I won't have to worry. But I do. I worry what that means, and what he intends to do.

"You ready?"

"Where are we going?" I ask Leon as he enters the room with the doctor who has discharged me. I move from the bed to the wheelchair he's holding for me.

"Dalton has had your Dad's place sorted with furniture for us for the time being, but I'm ready to take you home anytime you are."

"Thank you, Leon, for everything." I grasp his hand and squeeze. I was unfair to him. This must be so difficult for him, and I don't know how I can fix that. "You don't have to stay, you know?" I offer meekly.

"Do you want me to go?" He sounds offended and that was not my intention.

"God, no. Of course not. I just know you have a life and work, and you've already done so much."

"Alex, you were nearly killed and you're sticking around here. Like hell am I leaving you here on your own."

I don't tell him I won't be on my own. I just smile up at the man who has been my best friend through the loneliest years of my life. I don't like the thought of going back to my childhood home, but I'd rather be there than in the center of town in a hotel.

---

Anxiety stiffens every muscle in my body as I get in the car. Crunching metal and the whistle of the wind as it was pulled through the smashed windows echo around my head, and I have to put the radio on to drown it out.

"Are you okay?" Leon asks, and I smile firmly. "I'll go slow, okay?"

"Okay."

We pull up at the house and Dalton is tying a big banner that says:

## Welcome sort of home, Mom.

A little laugh pulls from my chest. DJ bounds towards the car. He opens my door and throws his arms around me.

"I have my own room here, Mom." He beams at me. I

look over to Dalton who shrugs his shoulders.

Leon takes my arm and helps me across the lawn, but is quickly replaced by Dalton who wraps an arm around my waist and practically carries me towards the house.

"I wanted him to feel comfortable here," he informs me, opening the front door. My mouth drops open.

The inside looks like a completely different house. There's a scent of fresh paint and everything looks new and revitalized. There's brand new furniture including a huge TV on the wall above the fireplace.

The floors have been polished and now have huge rugs decorating them.

"How did you do all of this?" I ask, astonished.

"You'll be amazed what money can accomplish."

"But this must have cost a fortune

"It's nothing, Alex. You're my family."

"But I'm not staying here, Dalton, not for the long term."

I hate that he spent a fortune doing this place up when I plan to go home soon.

"We can talk about that."

"I can't be here with your uncle. I won't put DJ at risk."

He stares into my eyes for a few silent beats. "I would never risk either of you. Trust me, okay?"

I study his features and gaze into his blue beautiful, truthful eyes. "Okay."

"Mom!" DJ shouts from my old room.

I let Dalton help me go to him. The room is nothing like it used to be. It's been transformed into a kid's dream room. One wall is lined with guitars and my mouth drops. They must have cost more than a car. There are gadgets set up, including every games console available, and another huge TV on the wall. Dalton knows what I'm thinking because he defends himself before I even open my mouth.

"He's been through a lot. I just want him to feel comfortable. I missed a lot of birthdays." He shrugs, looking vulnerable. Holding my stomach, I reach up on my tiptoes and place my lips against his. He sighs into them and sends my head swirling.

"I need to go somewhere and I won't be back until tomorrow."

"Where?" I ask, and then feel nosy. Am I supposed to want to know or…? I've never really been in a relationship so I don't know where we stand.

"I need to go visit my Dad, but I'll be back tomorrow. Leon is going to stay and Six is across the street."

"Okay."

He grasps my face possessively, holding me captive in his gaze. "I'll be back as soon as I can, and when I am, we can do whatever you want, even if it's leaving here."

The warmth of his breath caresses over my lips before he closes the gap and kisses me softly. "I love you."

"I love you too."

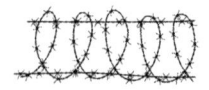

***

Sitting at the dinner table, everything feels fake, like we're sitting in a show home pretending to be a real family. We've sat like this so many times before, but now there's this atmosphere thick in the air that's suffocating.

"Mom, can I go now?" DJ bounces in his chair, desperate to go to his room to play with his new stuff.

"Sure, baby."

"Yes!"

Leon's eyes follow DJ. I get up to clear the table but Leon's hand comes down on top of mine to stop me.

"I'll do it." I want to say no, it's fine, but it's not. I've overworked myself just moving around and I'm exhausted.

"I don't want to lose you."

I look over at him, my brow dipping in concern. "What?"

"I want you to pick me. Come home with me."

"Leon," I whisper, dropping my head.

He stands and kneels before me, taking my hands in his. "I know you don't feel that way about me, but you could if you tried."

I pull my hands from his. "Don't you think I've tried? Don't you think I know how amazing you are? I do and I would have given anything for the pain to have ceased and my heart opened up for you but it doesn't work on will."

"He hurt you so bad, Alex. I'd never hurt you."

"Love is painful, Leon. Real love worth having makes you feel, and sometimes feeling hurts. If it's not making you feel, then it's not enough."

"Love should heighten everything good in your life, not darken it."

"Sometimes that darkness is seeking out someone to shine light on it."

Stunning me, he leans up and takes my mouth with his. Pulling away I stare down at him. "Leon."

He gets to his feet and leaves, slamming the door behind him. My heart aches knowing it's going to take time for him to heal and for us to get back to where we were.

---

I watch DJ from the doorway of his room as he strums one of the guitars Dalton bought him.

"I know you're there, Mom," he says, making me smile.

"Hey, baby. That sounds amazing."

"Meh, it needs work."

Pride overflows inside me. He's talented way beyond his years and has such dedication for music. I'm not sure where he gets that from but I'm happy he has it because listening to him is one of my favorite things in the world, along with the sound of his heart beat when he comes for cuddles in the mornings.

"Do you like this room?" I ask, and he shrugs and fiddles with the strings. "I'm sorry you had to meet your Dad the way you did," I tell him sincerely.

I told him his Dad went away and that wasn't a lie, but I didn't tell him where or that he was back. I didn't want him to ever think he wasn't wanted because even when I thought Dalton didn't want anything to do with him, I always wanted him.

"I like him." He looks up at me and offers a small smile that mirrors his father's.

"He likes you too, baby. Very much."

"Do you like him?"

I laugh and nod. "I love him very much. He gave me you."

## TEN

He puts the guitar down and gets up to wrap his arms around my waist. He's getting so tall that his head can rest on my chest now. "I want you to be happy, Mom."

I swallow the lump forming in my throat and squeeze him tight. "That's what I want for you too, buddy. I want you to tell me if this is all too soon and if you need time to get used to Dalton."

"He's my Dad, Mom. I want us to be a real family."

"I want that too."

---

Taking my painkillers, I lay down on the expensive-looking suede couch. I wake when I feel someone standing over me. My blood floods with ice and every hair on my body rises in fear.

# CHAPTER THIRTY-FOUR

*Demons*

## Alexandria

I sit bolt upright too fast, causing a tearing pain to shoot up my abdomen. "What are you doing here?"

He pushes a finger to his lips gesturing me to be quiet. He points towards the stairs. *DJ*.

"He looks like him," he says quietly.

"Get out!" I hiss.

He looks the same, only healthier. Older and fuller in the face. He has stubble but he looks clean and well kept. His dark eyes show the brother I knew in them.

"I came as soon as I heard." He points at the bruises healing on my face. "Those fucking bastards nearly killed you."

"Mom, is Dad back?" DJ calls out, and all my protective instincts tell me to go to him and keep him quiet.

"No, baby!" I call back, but I hear his footfalls.

I hold my hands out to Jonah, telling him not to move. I race to DJ and usher him back into his room. "It's no-one, baby, just the TV. It's time for you to get into bed."

"Already? But there's no school!" he whines.

"Mommy is so tired, baby. Please don't fight me on this."

He shrugs off his clothes and opens one of the drawers, which is filled with nightwear. He pulls on some sweat pants and jumps under the covers. I pick up his headphones and place them on his head. "Stay in bed now, baby, okay?"

He nods.

My finger itches to go for the phone and call Dalton but some deep-rooted bond I once had with Jonah stops me. What if Dalton kills him? Could I live with myself? Could I live with him?

"What are doing here, Jonah? You do know that Keith wants to kill you?"

"Fuck him." He walks over to the window and looks outside. "Is Mom here?"

"No. I sent her away when I found out what you guys did to Dalton."

He laughs but it's more sickening than comical. "I lost everything anyway. That wasn't how I wanted things to go."

"You let Dalton take the fall for you."

"Keith let him take the fall." He turns and anger swirls in his dark eyes.

"What do you mean?"

"I mean a Moore needed to go down. I didn't choose which Moore."

"Oh my God. Why didn't you tell Dalton? Why did you let it be him?"

"Let's not pretend I had any power there, Alex. They could have killed me."

"Dalton was your best friend."

"He was also fucking my baby sister behind my back."

He comes closer, causing me to take a step back and hold my hands out. He shakes his head. "You're still holding that against me?"

I almost laugh. "Are you joking? You tried to rape me, Jonah."

He makes a *pfft* sound and waves his hands in the air in a manic hand gesture. "I wasn't myself. I would have never really done it."

"Where have you been all this time?"

He looks around the house before his eyes rest back on me. "Nowhere. Everywhere. I should have been there for you with the kid. You should have let me be there."

"His father should have been there. You robbed him of that."

"Moores don't know how to be fathers. He would have just fucked it up anyway."

"Why did you end up that way, Jonah? Why did you go to Keith and get involved in that life?"

"Because I found out my life was a lie." He pulls out a chair and slumps into it. "Our mother is a hypocrite and our father was a fool."

I sit down.

## TEN

"When I was eleven I fell out of Keith's tree trying to get your kite, do you remember?"

"Yeah. You broke your arm."

He looks down to the scar on his elbow and rubs away a phantom pain. "Mom went crazy when she found out where it happened. I didn't take much notice at first, but once Dad arrived at the hospital I heard them talking outside my cubicle." He laughs. "It was a freaking curtain not a soundproof wall."

"What did you hear?"

"Mom panicking that Keith lured me over there because he knew."

"Knew what?" I don't know if I'm ready for the answer but I'm also intrigued and need to hear it. He looks me dead in the eyes with no emotion. "That I'm his."

I gasp. "That can't be…"

"It is, and when you think about it, really think about it, I fucking look just like him. How he hasn't put two and two together I don't know. Maybe he has and doesn't give a fuck."

"Mom hates Keith."

He shakes his head at me like I'm stupid. "Too much, Alex. She fucking hated him too much for there not to be a story there."

Oh my God.

"Dad knew?" I ask, astonished.

"Dad always wanted her, apparently, and when she turned up at his doorstep, pregnant by the town asshole, he married her and said I was his."

"Oh my God. So you and Dalton are related." It's not a question, just me thinking out loud.

He stands, making me jump. "None of it matters now."

"Why did you come here then?"

"To see you and make sure you're okay."

There's a rustling and then a bang from outside, and all of a sudden the door flies open and people enter. Jonah tries to fight them off but they hit him with the butt of a gun. I can't move. I'm paralyzed in fear.

*DJ…DJ…DJ.*

"Hello again. Maybe we can finish what we started this time." Tim Moore licks his lips and then his fist connects with the side of my head and my world is sent spinning.

# Six

My energy is heightened knowing Alex is over the street with her kid, and Dalton is leaving for the night. He had words with his uncle but I don't trust that sleazy cockroach one bit. He's a man on a mission and he thinks he has something to prove. Men like him don't just let shit lie. He hates his nephew, hates that he dictates to him. It's clear in his mannerisms, in his eyes, in his actions. I've seen men like him before and they're power-hungry and have a mob mentality. Bully until people submit. I fucking hate bullies. I enjoyed killing those fuckers who hurt my girl. I ripped them from limb to limb and got a taste for blood when it coated every inch of me. I've just got out of prison but I'm not opposed to going back in for the right reason. Protecting Alex and honoring my friendship with Dalton is as good a reason as any.

I still remember when he first walked into my cell.

# TEN

His young, fresh face wary of everything, and rightly so. You hear people say, "I'm too pretty for prison". In his case that was true. He would have been eaten alive in there if it wasn't for his name and the fact he went in ready to protect himself. I admired that. He reminded me of myself. Men prey on the weak inside those walls. I preyed on their wariness. No one knew me or what I was in for, they just heard whispers and tales. So I kept myself a mystery. I looked every fucker in the eye and made a point of putting myself out there. If anyone wanted to take a shot at me they would only get one chance, and no one did. The beast in me must be scarier than I think. But this kid, he didn't back down when I dared him to take back his pillow. He didn't try to get to know me and beg me to help him out when some cunt picked a fight with him in the shower. He was looking after him, letting people know he was there to do his time and he would do whatever he had to to make it out the other side. He didn't flaunt his father's name around when his Dad was in solitary. I liked him, and opened up to him. Men like him, if they're weak in prison, end up becoming someone's plaything. or they get their pretty face cut up from jealous fuckers. He came out just as pretty as he went in… on the outside anyway.

He came out my brother, and I'd do anything for him. I didn't hesitate when those fuckers came for me.

I saw them outside my window approaching Alex's house. Fuckers.

Grabbing the meat tenderizer I'd been using to soften up a slab of steak, I open the front door to be pushed back by a herd of men coming through. A shot rings out and a burning, shooting pain slices through my thigh.

Motherfucker shot me! I grin at him as I crack him on the forehead with the tenderizer in my hand. It leaves a nice pattern in blood on his face. I grab the gun, shove it under his chin and pull the trigger. It all happens so fast that they're still in the process of coming through the door, and I have them bottlenecked in the passage way. Brain matter sprays up the wall from my close range shot at the prick who shot me. His body falls, tripping the next idiot over. I stamp my foot down on his head while I grab and hit the fucker pointing his gun at me across the wrist with the meat tenderizer. His gun flies from his hand and he shouts from the pain as he tries to fight his way in, but comes up against my head connecting with his nose.

I bring my foot down a couple more times on the head of the guy that fell over, and relish in my boot penetrating past the skull. I bend down and grab the gun from his limp hand. Raising it, I shoot two rounds into the head of the guy who was too busy holding his face together to notice the gun.

The last guy manages to get a couple of rounds off, shooting me in the shoulder and hip. I fall to the ground but fire back a few rounds, which sends him running. The fire burns in my veins, the blood and bodies around me fueling the animal inside. I force myself up and give chase, the adrenaline pumping through me like a hit of the perfect drug. I can't feel the holes littering my body right now, all I can feel is the fucking rage of letting this bastard do any damage. I jump him from behind, sending him face first into the grass, his gun going a good eight feet away from him. I straddle him and he bucks underneath me like a wild boar. I help him turn around so I can straddle his chest, and lay a couple of punches to his face.

"He won't let you walk away from this!" he bellows at me.

I grin down at him. "And I won't let you." I push my thumbs into his eye sockets until the pop harmonizes with his screams. I push in deeper until he stops squirming beneath me.

Getting back to my feet, I wipe the flesh from my fingers down my tee and notice Alex's door is wide open. Those fuckers were sent to kill or distract me, and the latter worked. I rush over and enter the house to find the remnants of a struggle. My head rushes a little and a woozy feeling overcomes me. I rush down to the bathroom and splash my face with cold water. I pull open the cabinet and loads of shit falls out, including Alex's pain medication. I pop the lid and swallow a mouthful. I tear a strip from the bloodied shirt I have on and tie it around my thigh to stem the bleeding. My shoulder and hip will need something else. I check the wound and see that they're both through and through. This isn't my first rodeo. A lot of people get shot when they're part of a gang, and initiation into some requires you to take a bullet. Yeah, I didn't say I'm sane.

I make my way to the oven and light one of the burners. I pull at the drawers until I find the one with cutlery inside and grab a spoon, placing it on the fire. Unbuckling my belt and lowering my jeans, I pinch the wound on my hip to make it smaller and then use the burning spoon to seal the wound. It hurts like a motherfucker and I bite into my lip, drawing blood, but it needs to be closed or I'll lose too much blood. I repeat with the wound on my shoulder and thigh, and nearly lose it when I hear someone behind me. I grab a knife and turn quickly to find DJ standing a few feet away, staring around the kitchen. When his eyes land on me and the blood coating every fucking inch of me, his eyes widen and his bare feet shuffle backwards.

Dropping the knife, I lift my hands in surrender. "Hey, bud," I say in the least menacing tone I can muster. "Do you remember me?" I ask, feeling like a jackass. He has seen me a few times this week with his Dad.

"Where's my Mom?"

"I don't know, bud, but I'm going to find her, okay?"

"Is that your blood?" he asks, pointing to my apparel.

I don't know how Dalton would handle this but he looks old enough to not be lied to so I go with the truth. "Some of it is, some of it isn't."

"Is it my Mom's?" His face crumbles and I'm lost. I don't know how to handle him.

"No. I would never hurt your Mom or you. Okay?"

He nods.

"We need to get out of here now, okay?"

"Okay."

Sirens blare in the distance but I can't be sure that it'll be to help. I need to get Dalton's kid safe, and the only place I can think of is at the hotel with his grandma. Dalton had told me that the mother was still lurking around despite Alex telling her to leave, and at the moment, she's the only person DJ has that he knows and trusts, so she's going to have to do. I rummage in my jeans for my car keys and throw them to the kid. "You know how to drive, right?"

He looks down at the keys and then back up to me.

# TEN

"I'm nine."

I stare at him for a second. "So no?"

He hands me back the keys and grabs his coat.

---

The reception lady at the front desk of the hotel is freaking out at my appearance and threatening to call the police. I don't want to cause a scene or hurt her, I don't like hurting women, but I don't have time for this shit.

"Call up for…." I look at the kid. "What's your nana's name, kid?"

"Grandma." He shrugs like it's obvious.

"DJ?" a shrill voice calls out, and an older woman comes rushing over and grabs the kid away from my side. She stares at me wide-eyed and her arm flays at the receptionist. "Call the police," she demands.

"Fucking charming, bitch. I brought him to you."

"Where's his mother?" she demands, but I don't have answers for her so I leave before the law turns up and carts me away.

I'm limping now from the hip and leg wound and it won't be long before it renders me useless. I need to find her as soon as possible.

# Chapter Thirty-Five

*No*

## Alexandria

My head is thundering; there's a tropical storm causing chaos inside my skull. My eyes flicker open and I try to pull my hands to cover my eyes from the intrusive light burning into them but I can't move them. I'm bound. Terror courses through me. I'm cold and a light breeze blows over my skin. I'm spread-eagled on a pool table, naked. A cry rips from my gut. Those bastards. I'm fully exposed and completely vulnerable in the worst way possible. There are three of them; Tim, Keith and another guy, standing around, looking at me. I hear a commotion in the corner and squint past the tears to see Jonah tied to a chair. He's hurt bad and I know this is it; this is the revenge they so badly wanted.

"Glad you could join us. I thought we were going to have to have all the fun with a corpse," Tim teases, leaning down and sniffing at my hair.

"Fuck you." I gather the phlegm in my mouth and spit at him. He rewards me with a backhanded slap that sets a blaze across my cheek.

"Leave her alone, you motherfucker!" Jonah growls, wriggling in his chair. The gun shot rings out into the room, making me scream. Jonah calls out in agony. Keith shot him in the knee cap. He then walks over to me and places the point of the gun to my breast; it scalds, burning the sensitive flesh. I cry out and want to vomit at the smile on his face.

"Women. You were my brother's weakness too. Like father, like son."

"She has nothing to do with this," Jonah pants out with a broken breath.

"Collateral damage. She will be an example for others. You see, we're taking back our business and we want everyone to know what happens when you fuck with us."

"She's practically a Moore. Isn't there a family code or something?" Jonah laughs in an attempt to stall them from whatever they have planned for us.

"We've decided to weed out the rotten apples."

"Starting with Dalton," Tim chimes in. "That little fuck thought he could come out of prison and take over everything we built. He's fucking weak and pussy whipped, just like his Dad."

"His Dad won't let this happen," I say, trying to make sense of it all and what they are actually planning.

"He won't be around much longer, either."

Tim leans between my thighs and hits a ball with a pool cue. It hits me right between my legs and the pain and humiliation makes me sob.

"You know, they say a woman only feels four inches in." The cold tip of the cue parts my folds and I struggle and tell him to stop as Jonah goes wild in his chair. "Should we test that theory?" He pushes the cue inside me roughly. He goes too deep and the pain is excruciating. He pulls the cue back out and makes a face. "Oops. I guess I went too deep." He shows me the blood on the cue and then walks over to Jonah, wiping the cue across his cheek. "I'm going to fuck her to death and keep you around just long enough to watch the light leave her eyes."

Jonah struggles with the binds and then begins to cry and tell me he's sorry. Tim walks back over to me while Keith grabs Jonah's face and forces him to watch.

"You think she'll squeal for me like she does for Dalton?" Tim asks Keith, laughing. He unbuckles his trousers and reality that I'm going to be raped to death sets in. All I can think is, *'Don't let Dalton find my body and please never let DJ know how I died.'*

He climbs up on the table and over me. Bile burns up my throat and I have to turn my head to be sick so I don't choke and die, although that might be a better way to go. Tim's tongue comes out and licks at the tears rolling down my cheeks. "You look pretty when you cry, Alex."

"Fuck you"

"Oh, you're about to."

Another shot rings out into the room and my eyes dart to Jonah, with fear that Keith has killed him, but they're both staring at someone behind me. The sound of something hitting the floor draws my eyes and I see the other man that was with Keith and Tim lying on the floor with a bullet hole in his head. A couple more shots ring out and Keith goes down. Tim is panicking to get off me as feet approach the table. Six comes into view and I sob with relief and complete mortification that he's seeing me like this.

"Like to rape women, do you?" He drags Tim backwards from on top of me and then Tim's head hits the table between my legs. "Let's see how you like it."

Six grabs the pool cue next to me and snaps it over his knee. Tim starts struggling but Six quickly restrains him by grabbing him by the neck and shoving his face into the table. I hear a crack and know it's more than likely Tim's cheekbone. Six goes behind Tim and I see him ram the broken cue into Tim, who's still exposed from trying to rape me. The scream from him is like nothing I've ever heard before. Six doesn't stop. He rams the cue in and out and more sick spurts out of my mouth. Six releases Tim and he falls to the floor. Taking the bloodied cue, Six raises it up and then brings it down. I can't see them but I hear the squelch as it impacts a part of Tim's body.

"Watch out!" Jonah shouts, but it's not quick enough. Keith gets off a shot from the floor, wounding Six and sending him stumbling back until he falls to the floor.

The door crashes open and Dalton comes rushing in holding a gun.

# CHAPTER THIRTY-SIX

*Bye Father*

## Dalton

I came in to the bar this morning to find Jude waiting for me. I questioned where the hell he'd been all this time and he just shrugged at me and told me my Dad wanted to see me. When I questioned how the fuck he would know that he informed me that he works for my Dad and is there watching over me for him. I laughed, thinking he was joking, but his face didn't flinch; he was serious. Jude was there to look out for me? No, he was there to report back to my Dad like a little snake. I should have known something wasn't right when he started creeping around the place and asking for work. He'd never really been interested in the family thing, he was one to stay in the background and *observe!*

Damn it, how could I miss that? He had been away travelling and shit when I was finishing up my final year of school. I didn't even think he knew much about my father.

I'd had decorators and furnishers in and out of Alex's old place the last few days, making it livable for her and my son. I didn't want her to have any reason to go back with Leon. He had been a good sport this week but I could tell he hated being around me with a passion, and I couldn't blame him. I didn't like being around him either, but at least I got to have Alex when all was said and done. He's friend-zoned and can only watch her from the outskirts of her life. I can't be around her all the time if I can't be with her. It would slowly kill me, and it will kill him too if he doesn't find a way to move on. He's great with DJ though, and DJ appears to love him a lot, so for them I will tolerate him hovering. I don't really have the right to be all caveman on the guy, but it comes without permission, and fuck it, I'm a man and we can be possessive bastards.

Before she arrived from the hospital I had DJ make her a sign while I spoke with Six. He was strung real tight these last couple of days. I think a man like him senses something in the air when shit's about to go down.

"I need to go see my Dad. I need to discuss my uncle with him and let him know I'm out of all of it."

"He won't let you go easily." He clicks his neck and folds his arms over his chest. He is menacing as fuck and I'm grateful to have him more than he knows. I plan to sign the bar over to him so he can have his shop still when all this is done. I have enough money in the offshore accounts to last me and Alex a lifetime, and I see it as payment for 'time spent'.

"I'll watch over them. I won't let harm come to them."

"Thank you, brother." I grasp his bicep and he mimics my actions.

---

My knee bounced as I waited for my Father, the drive here was an anxious one and all I wanted to do was turn around and go back to Alex and DJ. It made me all kinds of uncomfortable being here in the waiting/visiting area of the prison. I felt like they were going to lock the doors and laugh at me, telling me getting out was just a joke and that I'm not really free. The smell and sight literally made my gut ache. I hated that I was there and not at home where I was needed.

But I had to know what he wanted; I needed to know that he knew from my own mouth that I'm done.

He walked towards me and I noticed the creases in his skin making him look older than his years. He was still a handsome man, but the inside has taken its toll on him, he walks with a hunch to his shoulders and there's that dead look in his eye that tells me there's a soul missing inside him.

"Your uncle has to go," were the first words out of his mouth. "He put a hit on me."

"How do you know that?"

"Don't question me, boy, or how I know. I know who and I'm going to kill him but you need to end Keith. Either you will or Jude will."

## TEN

I couldn't tell him about the case Jimmy has against my uncle. More than anything my Dad hates the law, and if I spilled what I know, he could do a one-eighty and inform Keith about what's happening. "It's not just me, kid."

"What's not just you?"

"He wants you gone too."

I always knew he didn't want me around. It wasn't a surprise and hopefully it wouldn't be a problem soon.

"I've told Jude to take care of him but it would be in better standing if you did it."

"Jude?" I ask. Jude is not capable of murder. He is a lackey, a bar runner, not a fucking murderer.

"Jude will get it done. He's promised me he will if you can't."

*Oh that's comforting.* "

"In the meantime you need to let her go, son."

"What are you talking about?"

"The fucking girl! She's not right for you, she holds too much power over you. She'll be your downfall."

"I'm out, Dad. This life was never meant for me. My name was my downfall, not a woman. Mom wasn't yours either. You were hers. You infect everyone around you and I don't want to be that. I don't want that legacy for my kid."

"Your kid?"

"I'm done. Bye, Dad."

"Ten! Ten! Dalton, come back here. Dalton!"

I gasped at the clean air when I made it beyond those walls, and jumped in the car. I wasn't going to stay, I was going to drive back, collect Alex and DJ, and get the hell out of dodge until Jimmy executed his plan and got my uncle put away.

My father wouldn't take what happened in there lying down, but if he sent Jude after me I was sure I could handle it. *Fucking Jude.*

The journey was spent breaking the speed limit, but the roads were quiet and everyone drives at their own speed anyway. The cop cars only go up to a certain speed and if they think they can't catch you, they don't even try. My pulse began to pound when I got to Alex's street and saw the flashing lights. I was shaking when I stepped out of the car and saw my old house lined with policemen who were stretching tape around the perimeter. The front door was open and the light shining from inside highlighted blood spatter up the walls. All the heat drained from my body as ice washed through me. It was like slow motion. I could hear and see everyone but I wasn't really registering them. There was a blanket placed over a figure on the grass. I rushed towards it but was held back by officers. I struggled to break free but when my eyes slid to the other side of the road I saw police in Alex's house. I ripped myself from the officer's hold and sprinted across the street. They tried to hold me back but Jimmy was there and he gestured for them to let me through. I rushed up the stairs and saw the house was a mess.

"Is she in there?" I managed to choke out, grabbing onto the door frame to stop myself from collapsing. *I shouldn't have left her.*

"There's been a struggle and we have found blood but no-one is here."

*Blood.*

## TEN

Fear planted itself inside my chest and weaved through my being, polluting my insides.

"DJ," I whispered.

"We've had a report that a man fitting the description of Taylor Jake entered the Mayflower Hotel with a boy who my officer on the scene has confirmed as a Dalton Junior Moore. Apparently he took him there to his grandmother and was gone before my officer got there."

"They don't have him?"

Jimmy shook his head and reached out to place a hand on my shoulder. "We have carnage across the street. Four dead and they are Keith's men, including little Harry Moore."

*Harry*. He was only twenty. He was Aunt Mary's only child.

"Do you have any idea where Keith would take Alex?" he asked me, and the reality that Keith had Alex burned into me like a red hot fucking poker to the heart.

"I need to go." I pushed off the doorframe and made my way back to my car, with Jimmy calling out for me not to do this alone.

Keith had to die. There was no other way he would ever let us be. If he'd harmed Alex in anyway, it wouldn't be quick.

I slammed the car door closed and opened the glove compartment to grab my Glock pistol. I placed it on my thigh and made my way to the bar. It was where Six would go and I needed to find out what he knew.

If he had DJ, he might have Alex too.

*Please let him have Alex.*

# CHAPTER THIRTY-SEVEN

*Sick*

## Dalton

I hear gun shots as I walk up to the entrance of the bar. The lights are on inside when I shut them all down. I could be walking into a trap but I can't not go in. I psych myself up to ready myself, and crash through the door, holding my gun out in front of me. My eyes can't take everything in. I locate my uncle on the floor next to a chair that has some bloodied up man in it. *It's Jonah.*

I wait for the hate to demand retribution but my heart fucking shatters and disintegrates into black ash when I see my girl tied to the pool table. She's naked and crying. I rush to her, keeping my gun on Keith who's struggling to raise his on me.

## TEN

"Dalton," she sobs, and I want to cry with her.

Her bruised and battered body from the wreck exposes the scar from her surgery. It looks angry and is seeping blood. There's sick in her hair and down the side of her face.

What the fuck did they do to her? I pull at the restraints, loosening them while keeping my eye on Keith. When I get down to her feet, I see Tim with his trousers down and a snooker cue through his eye. I turn to look back at Alex and my eyes travel up between her thighs.

No, no, no. There's blood there. I point the gun at the body of Tim and shoot.

"ARGHHHHHHHH"

"Dalton! Dalton!" Alex cries out, trying to cover herself with the arms I've just freed. I use my forearm to wipe the tears from my face and continue to free her legs. Keith is spitting blood and laughing at me.

As soon as her legs are free, she climbs into me and breaks, her body shaking with so much force I'm frightened she will fragment and never go back together.

"My jacket, baby. Take my jacket," I tell her, slipping it off while keeping Keith pinned with the barrel of the gun.

She grabs at it, wrapping it around her body, and then she runs to something behind me. I chance a quick look and see Six lying unconscious on the floor, bleeding. She checks his pulse and lifts his head into her lap.

"I told him I'd kill him." Keith nods to Six.

I look over at Six again and Alex nods and whispers, "There's a pulse."

"Looks like you didn't kill him."

"Doesn't matter now, anyway. We got Jonah. Help me

up." He clearly has lost too much blood if he thinks I'm going to help him to his feet.

"He is the traitor," Keith growls, and Jonah stirs in the chair.

"You're the traitor! You chose Dalton over yourself." Jonah leans forward and spits blood to the floor. He's in bad shape and looks too fucking white.

"Shut up!" Keith shouts, and before I can react to what's happening he points the gun and fires. Jonah's head flies backwards and Alex's screams whip through the air like lightning. I feel her body push past mine and take the gun from my hand. Shots ring out as she blasts the gun at Keith. He drops his gun and his body convulses. My gun falls from her hand and clanks on the floor as she runs to her brother and cradles him to her chest.

I run to Keith and scoot the gun away from him. I don't want the fucker having any more chances at pulling that trigger. Blood pumps from his mouth and he gurgles, trying to say something.

I lean down to watch the light leave his eyes. "Your Dad chose you to take the fall, not me," he manages to wheeze out, and smiles before all the air leaves his lungs. *My Dad?*

*"This will be the best education you can get Dalton, being inside will teach you things you could never learn out there. It toughens you up and prepares you for our life style"*

Bastard.

Sirens blast in the distance and red and blue lights

## TEN

dance through the windows as a barrage of armed police come through the front and back door. They point their guns at me and I'm forced to my knees and watch in a numb state as Alex is dragged from her brother's dead body and covered with a blanket. Voices call out and paramedics enter, rushing to Six. There's blood and bodies; it looks like a scene from a horror movie.

Jimmy runs inside and sees the carnage. His mouth is moving but I can't hear anything he's saying. I blink a few times when I see Jude next to him, and they're talking. Jude has a badge on his hip. What the hell?

"Dalton, look at me!" Jimmy shouts, clicking his fingers in my face. "They're going to take the cuffs off, okay? Keep it together."

I nod and he okays the officers to release me.

"Not how I wanted this to go down," he assures me. "Come on. I'll take you to Alex; she's going to need you. They sedated her for her own safety. This is going to take some getting over."

# Chapter Thirty-Eight

## *Burying Old Friends*

Dalton

*One Month Later*

I don't feel like I should be here after spending ten years fantasizing about him being dead, but in the end he was Alex's brother and my best friend, manipulated by a man he wanted approval or attention from. We will never know if Keith knew he was Jonah's father when he killed him. Alex's Mom had a nervous breakdown at the news about Jonah, and was hospitalized for two weeks. Alex suffered some minor internal injuries but she was released two days later from hospital. She will need therapy - a fucking shit load of it - but

## TEN

she's the strongest woman I know.

Her hand releases from mine as she steps forward to drop her rose into the grave. They take longer to release the bodies of those murdered so we're only now getting to bury Jonah.

Jimmy had already called in the cavalry for raiding the truck yard that night. Hence all the back up at our houses and the bar. They seized the truck yard and all its assets. Turns out Jimmy had been making a case for two years against Keith, and when I came out, he planted Jude to find out my role within the operation. Jude played my father and me. He played everyone. The two years travel he took after school was really for him to train as an undercover detective. His Mom knew, but no one else. He was the inside guy Jimmy was talking about. I know I got lucky. Jimmy cut me a big fucking break and it's not something I will ever forget. Jude had Dad on conspiracy to commit murder, hiring him to commit murder amongst, and a long list of other shit that totaled his sentence up to the point where he will never see outside those cell walls.

Six is made of fucking steel. That motherfucker took five bullets protecting my family. He spent three weeks in a coma and is now in a special treatment part of the hospital for physical therapy on his hip and leg.

He claimed self-defense for the murders he committed and the evidence was there to prove it. He had no charges brought against him, even if his methods did make a few of the officers sick.

I owe him everything. I signed the bar over to him and left him the house as well. I don't want any of it. Me,

Alex, and DJ are going to start fresh and finally live our lives.

# EPILOGUE

## Soul Mates

## Alexandria

His scent wraps around me, cocooning me in his embrace. The sun is up and the room is flooded with its glow. I love waking up to the crashing of the waves. This is our second honeymoon. On the first one, we took DJ with us, not ready to be apart from him, but it's been five years now and he's away with his hockey team at a training camp for three weeks, so we decided to make the most of it.

"Can we discuss this baby number two now?" Dalton growls in my ear before kissing down my body. He takes his time over my scars, taking extra care to kiss every inch.

"That's not discussing." I giggle. "That's getting straight

to making."

"You know I like to skip to the good bits, baby."

He grips my panties and slides them down my body. "When did you put these back on?" he asks, nibbling at the sensitive flesh beneath them.

"When I had to pee in the night."

"You pee too much lately," he says, and then swipes his tongue between my folds, eliciting a moan from my lips, and my back lifts off the bed.

"Mmm. Maybe I like to skip parts too."

His tongue swirls around my clit sending electricity flooding through my veins.

"What parts do you like to skip, baby? Because it isn't this bit." He pushed my thighs farther apart and teased my opening with his fingers.

"Maybe I skipped straight to being pregnant." I wriggle to try and get him to push those delicious fingers inside me.

His head leaves the warmth of my thighs and I groan at the loss.

"Baby?" His tone is serious.

I look down at him and run my fingers through his hair. I found out yesterday. I bite my lip waiting for his response. He looks down at my stomach like it's going to grow all of a sudden and show him I'm telling the truth. "My baby is in there?"

I tug his hair, forcing him to crawl up my body so his face is looking down on mine.

"Really? Are you really pregnant?"

I nod, smiling, and watch his stunning eyes fill with tears.

## TEN

He drops low to my stomach and kisses over my belly button. "Daddy is a stud! I didn't even have to try, baby," he tells my stomach, stroking his hands over the skin. All of a sudden his head pops up and concern draws his eyebrows together. "We still get to do the discussing stuff though, right?" He looks genuinely worried. I grab his face and tug him back up to me so I can kiss his lips. "If you mean the sex then, absolutely yes."

---

"This is heaven, being here with you like this. I don't ever want to get dressed," I say.

"If I've died or I'm going to die, I want it to be drowning in your kisses or suffocating by your thighs. When I go, I want it to be because you loved me to death or fucked me to death. Either or. "

I slap his arm and giggle.

"We can't control when we die but we can control how we live, and who we live with and I choose you. I will always choose you," I murmur my wedding vow to him.

"We will always be two hearts with one beat, two minds with one thought," he whispers.

In sync we both say:

"She was made for me."

"He was made for me."

"Soul mates."

COMING NEXT FROM
THE MEN BY NUMBERS SERIES

# SIX
## MEN BY NUMBERS SERIES

I grew up in the foster system and bounced around from place to place. I know what you're thinking. Bad things happened to me and fucked me up? Don't feel bad for me. I didn't know a privileged life, therefore I didn't miss one. I was what I was and I made it work. I actually had a few good homes in my lifetime, met some good people, but that's not what my story's about. It's not a Romeo and Juliet saga either, even if our stories do revolve around a similar basis. I knew a real love, a rare love, a love between two people that were never supposed to fall in love. Rival gang members are never allowed to fall in love and it cost us everything. The things I learned growing up the way I did is this: Love is deadly and often not real. People come and go and only the rare few stick around when shit gets tough. I learned the hard way what lurks behind false smiles, and deceitful truths get whispered in sexual moans. I was taught that dark souls are not born but created, and you can avoid them, hide from them or learn and become them.

Revenge sculpted and molded me into the darkest of souls, and with my wrath comes agony and torment more severe than hell itself. I took out six of the men who hurt my woman and I will be coming for the rest. Get in my way and I'll come for you too.

Coming soon by Authors
KER DUKEY and D.H.SIDEBOTTOM.

# Lost

BLURB

We came from nothing and were given a second chance at life, and life was pretty good until it tipped on its axis and my world came tumbling down around me.

My Baby Sister is missing…
Stolen…
Lost…

I've never felt this helpless before now, the vacant hole inside me expanding with each passing second of not knowing where she is.
What's she going through?
Is she hurt?
Suffering?
Alive?

The more I learn of her disappearance the more fear implants itself inside my heart, hardening - darkening.
The world is a depraved place, full of evil lurking behind normality.

Behind smiles.
Behind deception and facades.
She needs me and I will do whatever it takes to find her.
Whatever.
Whatever.

# Prologue

*Summer*

Summer has always been my favorite time of year, my mother must have known when naming me that I would seek out the sun, I craved the glow of its warm embrace on my face from as far back as I can remember.

    I also worshiped the feel of sand between my toes, the damp, soft touch as the weight of my body shifts the sand beneath them, the tips of the crashing waves teasing me with the cold promise of what the water holds. I even love the smell of the sun lotion soaking into my skin, but my most favourite part of summer… was that we always spent it together as a family and most of those days were spent at the beach. One of my favourite sounds in the whole world is the laughter of my big sister as she gives chase to me, scooping me up and spinning me around until we're both dizzy, the breeze sweeping our hair up and curling it weightless in the air like a floating leaf in autumn. The world distorting with each rotation until it's just us two in a whirlwind of innocence… of joy.

Those are the memories I go to, I hold on to, with a grip so fierce it numbs the reality of what my body is actually going through.

I didn't see my life ending up here…

All those dreams and possibilities, and now I would be remembered as just another statistic.

All the warnings from education, from Mom and my big sister Winter, and yet I still find myself here…stolen… lost.

Will they even look for me?

I look at the young girl battered and bruised in the bathtub, slung in there like garbage, her body broken, used up and destroyed. Matted hair that was once soft to touch, scabby lips that were once plump and pink, bruised skin that was once flawless.

Violated in ways no girl of her age should ever have to suffer.

Eyes wide, glassed over …dead.

This was my fate.

Coming soon

# The Forever Broken
## A Broken Novella

Blurb

Blaydon has been playing with fire when it comes to his best friends twin siblings, Quinn and Sofia. Sneaking behind everyone's back to be with them both, he finds himself struggling to choose between them. But maybe it's not a choice he gets to make.

When Sofia's troubles become too much for her to bear, will a desperate act force their truths into the light? Some secrets are used to cover even more painful deceits and they are about to cost them all immeasurably

COMING SOON FROM D.H.SIDEBOTTOM.

# Night Fires

I would watch him watch the ocean. He would build fires and sit, all night waiting.
For her. For his dead wife.
She never came. I never expected her to. But he did. And he never let go.
Even when I fell in love with him he never let go.
Until the night of the storm. The night my worst nightmares came to life.
And I lost everything to her when she finally returned.
                    For us both.

# ACKNOWLEDGMENTS

My readers:
Thank you for waiting! I know you've been dying to get your hands on this one and I kept you waiting… I hope you found it worth it. You amaze me with your support and love and make writing that much more special for me.

Special thanks to:
D.H.Sidebottom and Kirsty Moseley who keep me sane when I feel I'm losing it. Encourage and support is always supplied when I message them in melt down, I love you guys

Thank you to all the amazing Bloggers who help share this story. You guys are incredible and are appreciated more than you know:

stalKER'S :
Thank you for always having my back and pimping the shit out of everything Ker Dukey!

Terrie Arasin my PA, I love you fiercely and couldn't be me without you.

Stacey from Champagne formatting, thank you for always making time for me… even though I'm always in chaos.

Jillian Crouson, although we rarely get time to catch up, you always make time for me when I need you <3

THE PEOPLE THAT MAKE IT HAPPEN

Stacey – Champagne Formats
Kyra Lennon – Editor
Beta readers - Vicki Leaf, Charlie Chisholm
Proof reader – Jillian Crouson – Toth, D.H.Sidebottom
Cover photography – Clyph Jean-Philippe
Cover Model – Kyle Nelson
Cover design – Pink Ink Designs


Useful links
Find me here:


Facebook
www.facebook.com/KerDukeyauthor


Visit my website:
http://kerdukey.com/

Contact me here:
Ker: Kerryduke34@gmail.com
Ker's PA : terriesin@gmail.com

OTHER TITLES BY KER

**THE DECEPTION SERIES**
*FaCade*
*Cadence*
*Beneath Innocence - Novella*

**EMPATHY SERIES**
*Empathy*
*Desolate*

**THE BROKEN SERIES**
*The Broken*
*The Broken Parts Of Us*
*The Broken Tethers That Bind Us – Novella*
*The Forever Broken – A Broken Novella - coming soon*

**A STANDALONE NOVEL:**
*My Soul Keeper*

**THE BAD BLOOD SERIES**
*The Beats In Rift*
*The fire In Ice –TBA-*


*Lost – A stand alone novel*
*Coming soon*

Printed in Great Britain
by Amazon.co.uk, Ltd.,
Marston Gate.